THE DOGS
ON
MAIN STREET

CLIFFORD JAMES FAZZOLARI

*This book is dedicated to those who've shared
my Kingdom of Days on the way
to the Promised Land.*

Chapter 1 – Happy New Year!

Time to get another shitty year started, I thought as my feet hit the floor for the first time in 2012. No matter how many days passed it was difficult for me to imagine that I was living alone, in a beat-up three room apartment on the outskirts of Buffalo, New York.

It was actually my second New Year's Day in what had, by default, become my home. I thought of Rachael and how she had left me standing there, wondering what I was going to do with myself, after she had matter-of-factly announced that she'd had quite enough of me. She quoted Springsteen on her way out the door, and I really wish she hadn't done that because I repeated the verse in my head every morning, each day, before I even pulled my socks on.

Joe, I gotta' go. We had it once, we ain't got it anymore.

I sang the lyric to myself as I dressed for the first day of the year. All of my movements these days were pretty much automatic. I fished through a bowl on my dresser for the money it would take me to get the morning paper and a cup of coffee. I pulled on my filthy, black Carhartt coat and headed for the front door. There wasn't anyone for me to shout my intentions to, but I did it anyway.

"I'm going next door to get a paper!"

I was literally twenty-seven steps away from the Citgo combination gas station and quick mart that was my first stop each day. The wind whipped cold across the empty lot, and it dawned on me that perhaps the place was closed, but then I saw Rolando's huge frame moving in the front window. Before I even opened the door, I could smell the body odor coming from him. You see, Rolando was a lot like me. He just didn't care anymore. He was well beyond three spins. He very rarely changed his clothes, and despite the fact that he made a nice little living selling dope from his spot behind the counter, he didn't spend money on anything that would make him look even semi-presentable.

"Morning, Joe," Rolando said from his spot behind the counter. A roll of his belly fat was resting on the counter. As usual he had the racing form opened before him.

"Happy New Year," I said.

"Yeah, whoop-dee-fucking-doo," he said. He had a lit cigarette in the tray beside him despite the fact that he'd been threatened for the offense by New York State.

"Didn't give up smoking, I see," I said. "No resolutions this year?"

"I'm gonna' screw with even more people than I did last year," Rolando said. "I resolve to do just that."

Rolando took a long drag on the smoke and blew it out in circles above his humongous head. As usual his face was unshaven, his hair was greasy, and the Sabres tee-shirt he wore was ripped at the right shoulder. It was a hell of a New Year's outfit.

I grabbed a copy of the *Buffalo News* and worked my way to the coffee counter where I poured a cup as if I were in my own living room. After all, I'd been coming in every day since Rachael gave me the heave-ho and I moved into the shithole apartment across the way.

"You're out of milk," I said, shaking the empty pint.

"You know where it is," Rolando grunted.

I retrieved a new carton and headed back to the counter.

"You write your letter to your daughter yet?" Rolando asked.

"She's not my daughter. She's Dan's kid," I said. "But, it's the first thing on my agenda for the New Year."

Rolando knew all about my situation. He understood that losing Rachael had been bad enough but that I missed Anna even more. Anna was Rachael and her new husband Dan's daughter. In a way, she used to be my daughter, I supposed.

"That's so messed up," Rolando said. "The guy knocks her up and leaves her. She lives with you for eight fucking years then he comes back, starts up with her again, and takes *your* daughter away from you."

We had been over it way too many times. I filled a Styrofoam cup; three-quarters full with coffee, and then took my time adding milk and sugar.

"Life is a funny old thing," I said.

"But the dogs on Main Street howl," Rolando said.

"Because they understand," I finished.

Rolando folded the racing form, snubbed out his cigarette, and farted loudly.

"Jesus!" I yelled.

"Sorry, dude. I ate one of those frozen cheeseburgers about an hour back."

"So you aren't working on the diet for New Year's either?" I asked.

I was ready to approach the counter but the cloud rising from Rolando's back end was enough to keep me back for a moment.

"Light another cigarette, would you?" I asked.

Rolando obliged. I placed the coins on the counter. He reached across and pushed half of them back to me. "The coffee is on me," he said. "By the way, how many days has it been?"

For a split-second I'd forgotten our little game, but it came to me just as Rolando let another blast of gas loose. He wanted to know how many days it'd been since I'd been with a woman.

"Five-hundred-thirty-two," I said. "The glorious moment happened two months before she officially left."

I scooped up my change, tucked my paper under my left arm, and raised the coffee cup to my mouth, all the while stepping back away from Rolando and his magic gas.

"That's a long time to go between oil changes," he said. "You gotta' get back on the horse. Rachael is three-thousand miles away. She probably rode Dan's number for ten hours yesterday. Move on, buddy."

It occurred to me that perhaps I was sharing way too much with Rolando. He knew that Rachael and Dan had flown across the country with my blonde-hair, blue-eyed angel, Anna. He was also right, of course. Rachael wouldn't be doubling back from San Jose to make love to me anytime soon.

"I need to get started on my e-mail," I said. The thought of Anna made my heart ache. She'd be at the computer waiting on the letter from her bonus daddy. At least I hoped she would. Anna told me that she hated Dan almost as much as she hated California.

I opened the door and the cold air blasted through. The fresh air was good for the entire inside area of the store.

"Happy, happy, Rolando," I said.

"Say, wait a minute!" Rolando called out. "I saw something on the news last night."

I was half-in and half-out of the store.

"What's that?"

"Springsteen is going to tour the country this year. Are you going to chase him down, or what?"

I allowed the door to close. I tightened my grip on my coffee cup. Was Rolando messing with me? I hadn't heard anything about a new Bruce tour. After Clarence died, I figured they were through. How could they head back out on the road?

"Why are you messing with me?" I asked.

"I'm not!" Rolando said. "I bet its right there in your paper. It was on CNN or some other news channel. They hired a horn section or some bullshit. I can tell you one thing, I won't be going, but that won't stop you. Your life would be perfect if you could meet him, right?"

"I *am* going to meet him," I said. "We all are!"

"Never happen," Rolando said.

For nearly thirty years Springsteen had spoken to me at each and every important moment of my life. Rachael had chosen her parting words carefully, knowing that speaking Bruce lyrics to me would haunt me for the rest of my days. Rachael hated Bruce. It was a real sticking point in our relationship. It was actually what kept me from loving her completely.

"If he is on tour, I will meet him," I said. "This time out, I'm going to stand right before him and shake his hand. I'm going to tell him how much his words have meant to me. It's going to be my defining moment."

I felt myself getting emotional over the thought of breathing the same air as The Boss, instead of trying not to breathe in Rolando's digested cheeseburger.

"He'll have you arrested," Rolando said. "Stalking is illegal in all of the states."

But Rolando was dead wrong. Bruce would understand why I needed to shake his hand. Bruce himself had once staked out Elvis' mansion to catch a glimpse. Legend has it that Bruce had to do some fast talking to stop from being arrested.

"You made my year if you're telling me the truth about the tour," I said.

I swung the door open once more. The world outside the gas station door was bitterly cold as stray flakes of snow littered the air.

"Write the letter to Anna," Rolando said. "And Happy New Year, pal."

I wasn't sure if Rolando and I were pals, but I thanked him for the coffee, and resisted the urge to hug him. Was Bruce coming to Buffalo?

The door was nearly closed when Rolando's laugh and final words of teasing reached my ears, "The dogs on Main Street howl," he called out.

"Because they understand!" I yelled back.

I skipped out of the store and across the parking lot. Maybe 2012 wouldn't be quite as miserable as I thought.

I didn't even bother with the newspaper. Instead I turned on the computer all the while wondering why I hadn't been alerted by the Springsteen fan network that there was news about the tour. When the computer came to life, the alert flashed across my screen.

Springsteen announces tour plans!

It was true! My heart skipped a few beats as I quickly read the short article. Dates and venues were still being worked on, and there was a chance that it would start in Europe, but it was to be a full scale tour accompanied by a brand new collection of songs.

I jumped from the chair and blasted my fist high in the air. "Fuck yea!" I screamed.

For the next twenty minutes I scanned all the sites I knew that would provide information about Bruce, but there wasn't a lot more than the initial press release. Still, the short announcement had changed my plans for the day. There was so much to do. I would have to call Adam and Mary. We had pledged that we would meet Bruce on this tour, or we'd die trying, and now, the band was coming to a town near us!

"Yes! Yes! Fuck yes!" I screamed to my empty life.

Through the cloud of excitement, I thought of Anna once more. She would be waiting for my email. I clicked over to my mail account and brought up her name. I started the email as I always did.

"To my little baby girl!"

I wanted to launch right in on my news about Bruce, but instead, I tried a normal tone. Anna had tried hard to bridge the gap between Rachael and me.

"Can't you just *pretend* not to think about Bruce so much?" Anna had asked.

It was so hard to explain that Rachael didn't really hate me because I listened to Springsteen non-stop. There were certainly more pressing matters that caused the rift between us, but since Rachael didn't stop harping on me about it, perhaps that was how Anna saw it.

"Happy New Year!" I wrote. "This will be the greatest year of your life because if love is all you need, you have way too much, and that's because I love you more than anything that God ever created. I love you more than the moon and the sun and the stars. I love you more than Bruce."

I wanted to subtly break the news. I leaned back in the chair. This *was* going to be the year. I glanced up at the poster of Bruce from the *Devils & Dust* tour. I completely lost my train of thought as I considered some of the songs: *Maria's Bed, Leah, And Long Time Coming.*

"That's a great album," I whispered.

In the end, I decided to spare Anna from the news of the new tour. Instead, I wrote the inspirational quote of the day from an unknown author: *Be not afraid of tomorrow; for God is already there.*

I took a sip of coffee. It was already getting cold.

"Your word of the day is *vindictive*," I wrote. "Vindictive means being vengeful or showing ill will and a desire to hurt."

It was a strange word choice, but what had flashed on my computer screen this morning as the word of the day. I tried to explain it to Anna in a way that she'd understand.

"I can never be vindictive when I think of your Mom or Dan because they are the beautiful people that created you. I love you, Anna. Love always, your Bonus Daddy."

I hit the send button. I couldn't possibly love anyone more. Bruce and the boys would be touring soon. It promised to be the greatest year of my life.

Chapter 2 – Shit for Brains

One of the problems with losing at life is that I'm forced to complete menial tasks at a dead end job that has very little redeeming value. Despite the fact that the rest of the world was enjoying a long weekend as a result of the New Year's holiday I was up at out of bed early. My shift at the Target Department store started at 7 a.m., and if I punched in even a minute late I would be sitting in front of my boss, Lawrence Peacock, who is a pure asshole.

Peacock was the regional manager of the Northeast division of all the Target stores, and as far as I could tell his job was simply about power and control. He honestly didn't seem to care about much more than showing the staff that he was the boss and that we were all worthless. As if we didn't know.

Thankfully, I punched in seven minutes early. I was sure that Peacock wouldn't hand me a bonus check for doing so. In fact, the completely bald, anorexic-looking, wire-rimmed glasses, bad-breathed, douche bag was standing just outside the door to the break room.

"Joe, you're working on displays today. I want you to set-up the sales display at the front of the store. Make sure that your cart and materials are clear of the main aisle. We don't want someone tripping over your garbage and breaking their neck. Also, make sure you cut the boxes neatly. The last time you built a display it looked like a kindergarten kid displayed it."

"Happy New Year to you too!" I said.

I shuffled by him. He wasn't supposed to be handing out assignments and ridiculing the help, but he couldn't see fit to live any other way. Someday, when it all came together for me, I'd punch him right in the forehead. I often dreamed about imbedding his glasses to his face.

"Oh, right! Happy New Year," he said.

For the next half an hour I gathered materials. Since I hated every second of my job, building displays sucked ass. Yet it would minimize the time I spent talking to customers, as they struggled down the aisles trying to find crap that was right in front of their faces. I would be able to daydream about meeting up with Bruce and the E Street Band.

I was thirty-five minutes into the job of building a display of laundry detergent when my cell phone buzzed in the front pocket of my beautiful red smock that had the ever-annoying phrase, 'I'm here to help!' emblazoned across the front. I wasn't supposed to chat on the cell phone during working hours, but Peacock wasn't anywhere in sight, and Mary's name was on the display. I crouched down behind the hand truck that held fifty of the damn cases of detergent.

"Hey Mary! Did you hear?"

"Yes!!!" Mary screeched in my ear. "You remember the pact, right? We chase Bruce until we meet him!"

Mary was absolutely shouting into the phone. Now I admit that a 44-year-old man and a 48-year-old women chasing a rock star around the country might not seem like a plan for eternal salvation, but we had convinced ourselves that it would change our fortune. I knew that Mary was 100% behind the effort.

"They haven't announced any dates yet," Mary said. "But we have to get the plan in order. Have you talked to Adam?"

"Not yet," I said.

Out of the corner of my eye I saw Peacock heading my way. He was still at least a couple of hundred yards away, but he had confiscated my phone before, and it wasn't going to happen today. It was a brand new year.

"Listen, Mary, how about we meet at Starbucks at 3:30? I'm working until 3. I'll buy you a latte."

Mary agreed quickly, but as she started in on one of her spiritual rants I clicked the phone off and returned it to the safety of my frock. Peacock was closing in.

I cut open one of the boxes to show the detergent, and while it sounds easy, there have been times when I've cut into the plastic bottles and spilled detergent all over the floor. According to Peacock this was a cardinal sin because not only did I damage the product, but I also let slippery soap loose on an unsuspecting public that might slide on by. Asshole.

Peacock stood over the top of me. I was on my hands and aching knees, moving the heavy boxes here and there to set up the display.

"So far, so shit," Peacock said. "Why do all of the displays you put up tilt slightly to the left?"

I stood up slowly. Peacock's head was tilting back and forth as he tried to figure out how I got the seven boxes I'd stacked out of level. As I looked over my work, standing beside him, I could see that he was right. The third box in the stack was uneven, causing the rest to lilt to the left.

Peacock placed his left hand to the center of my back. Slowly, he moved his hand up to my neck and then he pushed ever so lightly on my neck until my head shifted to the right.

"There we go," he said. "It looks straight now."

"I'll fix it," I said.

Peacock let my head go, and then tapped the center of my chest with his clipboard. "Take pride in what you do," he said. "That's the secret of life. If you do that, you'll find that everything else falls into place."

Peacock started off to the front of the store. Perhaps, in hindsight, had I not stepped back to flip him the bird, the entire episode may not have happened, but my one step backwards proved to be a huge mistake.

The woman cried out as my leg made direct contact with the front leg of her walker. She tumbled over the top of the walker, I stumbled over the top of her, and we both crashed straight into the leaning cases of detergent.

"What the fuck!" I yelled.

Of course, the lid came undone on one of the bottles of detergent and there was a green flood of liquid heading for the front cash registers. Peacock, of course, was on his way back to the commotion.

I scrambled to my feet, which was no easy task as I slipped in the detergent. I reached for the old bag's hand, but she was pretending that her hip was broken. I wanted to scream, "Get the hell up!"

Peacock was there in a flash.

"Shit for brains!" he exclaimed. "You have shit where your brains are supposed to be!"

The woman was wailing as though she were being crucified. To be honest, she looked as if she were at least eighty, and the meeting with the ground must have been awfully unpleasant for her, but what the hell did I do? She barreled right into me.

An hour later, I was back in my apartment looking for more information about Bruce's tour. Peacock had fired me on the spot. I didn't even stick around to watch them load the old witch into the ambulance. Of course I hoped that she'd be okay, but what good does it do to say I'm sorry four hundred times in a row? Peacock was right. There was shit where my brains were supposed to be, but it was a town full of losers anyway, and I was pulling out of Target to win.

***

I had plenty of time to waste before I had to meet Mary at Starbucks so I tried to figure out my financial plan, and I wrote my daily email to Anna. I was a little disappointed that she hadn't responded to yesterday's note, but it was hard to get mad at a ten-year-old girl. There were more important things in her life, like her Mom and real Dad. The thought of Dan sent me headlong into a daydream of his death in a fiery one-car crash. I could almost visualize the first cop on the scene as he threw up into the bushes and told his partner, 'It's the worst thing I've ever seen.'

But, I knew that it wasn't right. Despite the fact that the man made half a million bucks a year and stole my family right out from under me, I wasn't going to be vindictive. Even though I couldn't stay out of my own way, I knew the right way to act. I just hoped that Dan could see fit to be man enough to treat Rachael and Anna with respect. I had done that much.

I started the email with the news of Bruce and the tour. Anna would see it on the television soon enough so I had to tell her how excited I was.

"Hi my little baby girl! Anna, I know that you don't really understand it, but I am so excited today because Bruce is going to tour again, and he has a new record out! Your Mom might say something funny about it, but just know that it makes me really happy. You see, when I was about 17, I saw Bruce in concert for the first time. It was at a place they call the Aud here in Buffalo. It was my first date and I was really nervous, but Bruce was so good that night that I really felt like it was the first time that I was actually alive! Now honey, I know that sounds weird, but when Bruce sings about standing up for yourself and respecting God and other people, it makes me feel good inside, and that's where it's important. No matter what happens in the outside world, no one can ever take away what's inside. So, our quote for the day is this: *A successful man is one who can lay a firm foundation with the bricks others have thrown at him.*

Anna, that was written by a man named David Brinkley. He is a smart guy. You should try and surround yourself with smart guys. If you fly with birds that fly backwards, sooner or later you'll be flying backwards too."

Our word of the day is *Voluminous* which means something that has great volume, fullness, size or number; ample or length in speech or writing; voluminous paperwork. Like Bruce Springsteen has a voluminous catalogue of written songs.

I love you, Anna. My love for you is stronger than the wind during a hurricane. I will never stop being your bonus Daddy."

I checked one more time to see if Anna had responded to yesterday's email. The inbox was empty. I thought about grabbing a soda at the Citgo so I could see what Rolando was up to, but instead, I threw on my *The Wild, the Innocent and the E Street Shuffle* and I listened to *Kitty's Back* and *New York City Serenade* about ten times each. By that time it was off to Starbucks and my meeting with Mary. It was about to get really interesting.

CHAPTER 3 – SO MARY CLIMB IN

My foray into college had lasted just a semester and a half. My father had screamed about the money that it cost him for me to earn three failing grades, two D's, and an A in creative writing at the University at Buffalo. Mary was my creative writing teacher that first semester back in 1986. She was also the woman who made me a man, as we had a couple of torrid sexual encounters. There was no way to have any other type of encounter with Mary. She was torrid in every encounter, sexual or otherwise. I loved her from the first moment I laid eyes upon her, but she could never be just mine. Mary belonged to the universe.

I had no way of knowing what transformation Mary would take as it had been seven months or so since we'd last met. Mary's appearance, most likely, changed fifty times since we last shared a cup of coffee.

I entered Starbucks slowly. I actually hated everything about the place except for the fact that their product was good. It would most likely cost me most of a ten dollar bill for two hot beverages, but it would be worth it. Mary would continue my education for me, and we'd be talking all things Bruce. Yet for some reason I was nervous.

My job was gone. My life was essentially all about this tour, and absolutely nothing else.

The line for coffee was long. I counted seven people in front of me at three o'clock in the afternoon. Laptop computers were opened all along the back wall and at the center table. The chatter was at a minimum as all eyes were on the computer screens. I did a quick scan of the faces peering at those screens and realized that Mary had not yet arrived, but she was always late anyway. Mary would enter the place in a flourish of scents and sounds, and every single head in the place would turn to her.

The line moved forward slowly. The girl directly in front of me appeared to be in her early twenties. She had long blonde hair and an extremely tight little figure. I stared at her ass for so long that she must have felt it burning. I didn't care. As I had it figured, she wanted me to look at it otherwise she would not have gotten a tattoo on her lower back or worn a shirt that kept riding up. She was wearing bright red thong underwear that sent my mind a reeling. As we moved forward one person, the girl glanced back at me. It's strange, but there is something about knowing that you're being watched, isn't there?

"Did it hurt?" I asked.

"I beg your pardon?"

"Your back tattoo, did it hurt?"

The girl pulled her shirt down a bit as though my looking at it had greatly offended her. She turned quickly and faced the front. She didn't even feel compelled to answer my direct question. Every ten seconds she yanked down on the back of her shirt. I kept looking at her ass anyway.

The door to the front entrance seemed to open differently. Don't ask me what the difference was, but I definitely heard it. Three seconds later, I was laughing as I took in the site of my former teacher and very first lover.

"Good morning patrons of capitalism!" Mary announced. Every single head turned to take in her approach, and what an approach it was. Mary was dressed like Lady Gaga with an array of scarves and jangling jewelry. Her hair was fire engine red, and the scent of some sort of mystical oils took control of the entire room. She made a beeline straight for me, and moaned loudly as I hugged her tightly. The small black beret that topped off her extravagant outfit shifted to the right.

"Let us always meet one another with a smile, for the smile is the beginning of love," she said. Her soft lips brushed my right cheek, my left cheek, and then my lips. "And I love you, so much, Joseph, my friend."

The girl with the ass and the thong turned and shot an annoyed glance in Mary's direction. She plugged her tiny button nose with two of her pointy little fingers.

"Good morning!" Mary said to the girl. "My, aren't you just plain beautiful!"

The girl smiled through a thoroughly confused look.

"Do you know my friend, Joseph?"

The girl shook Mary off and stepped up in line once more. We were just two people from the front where the men and women dressed in green filled the cups.

"You should take the time to know Joseph," Mary said. "He has the heart of a lion and the soul of an angel. He's a beautiful person inside and out, right Joseph?"

"I suppose," I said. Being beside Mary had ceased to be embarrassing a long time ago.

The girl really wanted no part of a continuing conversation with Mary, but turning your back on Mary rarely works.

"One little piece of knowledge for you," Mary said softly. "And then I will leave you alone."

The girl suddenly seemed trapped in the soothing manner of Mary's voice.

"This comes to you directly from the Dalai Lama. Do you know who the Dalai Lama is?"

The girl shook Mary off once more. Mary's constant smile was winning her over though.

"That's not important," she whispered. "The message is what is important. Just remember the wisdom. *If you want others to be happy practice compassion; if you want to be happy, practice compassion.*"

The poor girl was called to the front counter and she looked back at us again before she ordered a caramel coffee that was probably the only thing she'd put in her body all day. I couldn't help but laugh as I understood that Mary had made the exact impression that she wanted to make. The girl would not soon forget her time in line at Starbucks. The fact that we met the girl was summed up in Mary's next line, which was whispered in my left ear.

"She has a terrific ass, doesn't she?" Mary asked.

Ten minutes later we were seated at a booth in the back of the coffee house. It was from my spot behind my Chai tea latte that I got my first real good look at Mary. She still looked as if she were in her late twenties. There wasn't a single wrinkle on her pretty face, and the red hair brought out the true beauty of her green eyes. Mary had always dressed her eyes as if they were going to a debutante ball, telling me that the lamp of the soul was alive in the eyes.

"Bruuuuuuccccccceeeeeeee!!!!!" Mary wailed and every single head in the place turned in our direction.

"It's awesome!" I said. "Clarence won't be there, but it has to be great, right?"

Mary was already shaking me off. She sipped her tea and waved her right hand at me. The ten or so bracelets on her arm jangled.

"What makes you think Clarence won't be there?" she asked. "Is it because he died? Of course he'll be there! Clarence will be in every single seat in those arenas. We will hear the perfect melodies in every screech of Bruce's voice. We will see Clarence alive in the eyes of the ticket-takers, and the beer vendors. On this tour Clarence may be more alive than he has ever been! People fail to realize that the spirits survive and that there is no such thing as death. Sure, we won't be able to see him on that stage, but he'll be there. God knows! He'll be there! He'll be sitting with you and me and Adam."

Mary sipped her tea and smiled once more. I had so many questions for her. Was she still teaching? Was she still involved with the man who had tried, on numerous occasions to beat the spirit out of her? Did she still believe that God controlled all of our movements and that Bruce was actually a prophet who was sent to the world to take away some of our pain? I imagined that I knew all of the answers, but they would come to me slowly.

"Have you spoken with Adam?" she asked.

"You know how he is," I said. "He's probably sucking a beer under the sun, looking for someone new to bang so he can work off his hangover from last night. When you have as much money as Adam does life is just a gigantic party, right?"

"Adam is lonely and we both know that," Mary said. "He knows that a loving heart is the truest wisdom. He may need this tour more than either one of us."

The girl with the nice ass seemed awfully interested in our conversation. She was at the next table just a few feet away, pretending to sip her coffee, but listening to every word out of Mary's mouth.

"What's new in your life?" I asked, knowing that the answer could cause me to fall straight to the floor.

"Still living in the temple of tranquility," Mary said. "My life as a humanist has never been more rewarding than it is right now. Over the last few weeks I've been seriously contemplating starting a church. Would you be a member of my church?"

Mary's eyes were darting from me to the table where the young girl sat and back again. I knew that our encounter with perfect ass wasn't yet complete. Yet Mary didn't call out to the girl. Instead she reached across the table and grabbed my right hand, lovingly pulling it towards her. I was all for it. Mary studied the lines of my hand, tracing her long fingernails that were painted light blue, over each line.

"Oh, a lot of tension," she whispered. "You are having troubles with love, troubles with your work, and troubles in your heart."

"No shit," I said. "Wow, you're good!"

I laughed, but Mary didn't. Her brow furled in true concern. "Are you trying to discipline your mind like I taught you?"

"Everything's a mess," I said. "That's why I need Bruce so bad."

Mary was shaking me off. She caressed my hand softly, rubbing each knuckle gently, offering the calmness that seemed to permeate her whole body. It felt so good to be touched lovingly that I thought I might cry. As per usual I was absolutely entrapped in Mary's soothing manner. I closed my eyes, feeling a wave of comfort reach my heart, mind and the soul that Mary was always speaking of.

"The universe loves you," Mary whispered. "The true way is not through a man keeping count in the sky. The pure beauty of life is found in your perfect heart. Love deeply. Live peacefully. Love, Joseph, live, Joseph…love."

Mary continued to whisper the words to her prayer over and over again.

"I feel the negative energy leaving your soul," she said. "Your hand is warming to my touch. Love deeply. Live peacefully. Love, Joseph, live Joseph…love."

My trance was broken by a clearing of the throat. My eyes jutted open to see the girl with the perfect ass crouched at the table just mere inches from where Mary and I were connected by the hands. There were tears racing down the pretty girl's face.

"That is the most beautiful thing I've ever seen," she said to Mary. "The way that you touch him is unbelievable. I have never witnessed such love."

For the next thirty-five minutes Mary and I chatted with Layla. Yes, she had been named after the Eric Clapton song. No, she wasn't a fan of Springsteen, but she wanted to go with us as we followed him around the Northeastern part of the United States. The worst part of it all being that I had to spring for three more four-dollar hot beverages.

"My stepfather loves Bruce," Layla said, "And since I hate my stepfather maybe the best thing for me to do is to trap Bruce. I'll screw the Boss six ways to Sunday and rub my old man's face in it."

Yet Layla was a sad sack of a girl, if you asked me, and despite the fact that the longer I was in her company the more physically attractive she became, I didn't want her invading the group.

Mary was another story. She had a new student. As far as Mary were concerned the greater the handicap the better it felt to fix it.

"I'm lost," Layla said as she drained the last of her second caramel drink. "I tried school and it didn't work. I tried women a couple of times. I tried men over and over and over and over and they all turned out to be complete losers who were only interested in tapping my ass."

"Not all men are like that," Mary tried.

Layla turned to face me.

"Joseph, was it my ass that attracted you when we first met?"

I couldn't answer. I wanted to tell her that she decorated it like a Christmas tree to attract my attention, but I didn't.

"I rest my case. When do we leave to catch up with Bruce?"

We still didn't have a tour announcement, but her question put me front and center.

"My plan is to work about four or five cities into the mix," I said. "We'll see him in Buffalo, for sure, maybe Cleveland, Pittsburgh, Toronto and definitely New Jersey. We need to see how it all breaks out, but we should be able to make it to all of those. I figure that we drive, and with our computers and phones, and trying our best not to concentrate on anything else, we will eventually see Bruce face-to-face somewhere."

"And what do we do once we see him? How is he going to save our lives, exactly?" Layla asked.

This is where Mary stepped in. She waved a purple and green scarf in Layla's face.

"Bruce is a spiritual man with a heart of gold. Shaking his hand and telling him how much he means to us will be the culmination of a lot of events in our lives. We have all spun in circles trying to find our way, through all of these years, and the only link we truly shared was our appreciation for what he was trying to say. Like the characters in his songs, we have been traveling here and there, near and far, and we haven't yet quite grasped the brass ring. When we meet him, we will know! As crazy as it sounds, we will have the blueprint for the rest of our lives, right, Joseph?"

I simply smiled. The entire plan had been Mary's brainchild, from day one. I remember the very night back in 1983 when we had hatched the idea. Mary was naked in bed beside me. We were listening to *Born in the USA* and *Downbound Train* in particular.

"How many times have you seen Bruce?" Layla asked me.

"Twenty-seven," I said without hesitation. "The first time was back in 1983. There was actually one year when I saw him seven times."

"1983!!!" Layla shrieked. "I wasn't even a thought in my father's tiny little fucking mind then. I wasn't even born until 1990! Do you think I should go with you?" Layla asked Mary directly.

"T.S. Eliot once said: *Only those who risk going too far can possibly find out how far one can go.* I definitely think you should go. The temple of tranquility has another member!"

I turned my coffee mug over on my plate. I wasn't real sure how to digest such information, and my best guess was that we would never see Layla again.

"Listen," Mary said. "I have to get back to my home. My boyfriend is coming over and he certainly has rage issues. If I'm late arriving, he may snap."

It was the one thing in Mary's life that I never truly understood. Ralph was the man who beat her so badly one time that she spent eleven days in the hospital. Still she couldn't find it within her spiritual heart to leave him. We often joked that Ralph had been the true name of Bruce's character in *Johnny 99*, a song about violence and tragedy.

"Don't even start the lecture," Mary said. "Just get a hold of Adam. We have to get to the bottom of the logistics. We are going to need money and a vehicle, but we are all paying our own way. Make sure that Adam knows that we will have a set dollar amount. Mostly, we need a getaway plan."

We met outside the front door for one last lingering hug. I must admit that when I hugged Layla for the first time I held on way too tightly, and way too long.

"I told you he's thinking about my ass," Layla said to Mary when our embrace broke. "I will be a true asset in getting close to Bruce. I'll sleep with every dude who stands in our way."

Mary gave a great wave of her sash as she ambled towards her electric car. "I have a lot of work to do to save this poor girl," she said.

Mary climbed in her car. I watched her pull to the exit. Our lives would have been so much different had we been able to stay connected.

That night, I laid in my bed with *Darkness on the Edge of Town* the featured work for the evening. I sang the song *Something in the Night* over and over, but I didn't break into tears until I heard the title track. Bruce had been in a real bad way when he penned the lyrics to *Darkness on the Edge of Town*. I knew exactly of what he spoke. Life was a cold, hard ride, and despite seeing Mary and meeting Layla, I was awfully lonely. I missed Anna. I missed Rachael. I missed being alive.

"Hi my little baby girl! Just thinking of you tonight. How come you haven't written back? You're probably busy having fun! I hope so. Our quote of the day comes from Marie Curie. *Nothing in life is to be feared; it is only to be understood!* I love you my precious girl, and love is the best word I can think of for today's word of the day. You know what love is, right? It's all that I have in my heart for you! With love always, your bonus Daddy."

Chapter 4 – Adam Raised a Cain

I wasn't exactly sure why I set the alarm on my phone, but *Waitin'
on a Sunny Day* stirred me awake at five minutes to six. Normally
getting out of bed that early would allow me enough time to grab
the coffee and paper, shoot the shit with Rolando, and get ready for
work. I considered the fact that my job was really gone, and that
kicked me headlong into thoughts of how much money I had to
my name.

Rachael hadn't left me high and dry. Considering that Dan was
a big-shot, fucking money-grubbing bastard she could leave me
ten grand in our joint account and not worry about it too much.
Thankfully, she had done just that, but how long would ten grand
last? The trip would certainly cost us each plenty of money, but
Mary would want to do it on the bare minimum. I left myself a note
to ask Mary what she was thinking.

I gathered coins from my dresser slipped on a pair of black and
white pajama bottoms and a concert tee-shirt from the *Tunnel of
Love* tour. I thought of the fact that Bruce had been in the middle
of his divorce during that tour. I wondered how he handled such
a private moment in his public forum. I had screamed from the

highest heavens that he shouldn't marry a Hollywood actress, but what can you do?

The wind was whipping hard and there were snowflakes in the air, but we still weren't getting much in the way of winter. Buffalo weather had a way of turning quickly though, and we were always just an hour away from a lake effect snowstorm. It really was a miserable place to live when the shit started flying.

I opened the door to the gas station and the spot where Rolando usually stands was vacant.

"Yo, Fatman," I called out. Sometimes Rolando would lose track of time back on the toilet. I'd lecture him about the fact that I could steal what I want and never get caught. Rolando would always tell me that I was welcome to as many air fresheners I could steal as he took a dump.

"GET ON THE FUCKING FLOOR! NOW!!!"

I turned from the front counter to the back area where the coffeemaker was positioned. My eyes went from the gun to Rolando, who was as flat on his stomach as he could get. The man holding the gun was waving it manically. He was wearing a Halloween mask of George W. Bush. If it weren't for the gun, I might have laughed. Instead, I dropped to the floor as if he'd already shot me.

"How much money do you have on you?" the gunman asked.

I was glad that he wasn't yelling anymore. I thought about telling him to remain calm. My eyes went to Rolando's face. The big man honestly seemed to be disinterested. He shrugged.

"I only brought in enough for the paper and a cup of coffee," I said. I slid it across the floor to George W.'s feet. He bent to scoop it and I got a good look at the gun. I had actually owned a gun just like it once before. It shot b.b's.

"What the fuck! I got eleven dollars! I can't even rob a fucking place right."

The man made it to the front counter. He grabbed a handful of Slim Jim's and about a dozen packs of cigarettes. For good measure, he took the entire tree stand of air fresheners.

"This is bullshit!" he yelled.

The front door opened and shut. I couldn't help it, I started to laugh. It began as a slow giggle, but when Rolando joined in, it became a belly laugh.

"Good morning, buddy," I said.

"Can you believe it? He took the air fresheners!"

Rolando helped me up. He filled me in on the part of the robbery that I'd missed.

"I was in the back having my morning movement and reading about the fucking Sabres. I heard a noise and thought it was you so I didn't really rush it, but then the guy starts yelling out, 'Can I get some help out here!'"

Rolando poured two mugs of coffee as I reached for the milk.

"So I come out and there he is, George W. in all his glory! I started laughing, but when he showed me the gun I nearly had my second shit of the day. He was asking about the safe as if this is Fort Knox. I opened the register for him and then I got on the floor. That's when you came in."

"You do know that wasn't a real gun, don't you?"

Rolando looked a little confused for a split-second, but no one likes to admit that they got fooled. "Of course," he said. "But if someone needs something so bad I ain't gonna' stop them. I'll tell you one thing though I've had enough of this bullshit. I gotta' get out of this life."

"You can come on the road with us to chase down Bruce," I said.

For the first time, Rolando didn't just dismiss me out of hand. "Let me think about it," he said.

The rest of the morning was spent cleaning up my apartment, and trying to figure out the details of our adventure. Bruce and his staff weren't truly cooperating as there wasn't any new information offered regarding the tour. I was going to be in real trouble if the tour took the band all over Europe first. I didn't have a job, and I didn't care about anything enough to get the old drive in gear. Still, I cleaned, and every twenty minutes I dialed Adam's cell phone, hoping to make a connection.

Adam was the first guy I met on the University at Buffalo campus. We were destined to meet, but only because the administrators had assigned us to the same small room. While I was unpacking my clothes and making my bed, Adam made a grand entrance. He held a six-pack of Budweiser.

"Hey fuck-face, think fast," he said.

The can of Bud hit me in the side and bounced twice before escaping to the space between my bed and dresser. Adam tossed an Army duffel bag on the empty bed, and eyed me for a long moment.

"You don't want to drink with me?" he asked. There was a real pained look of hurt deep in his eyes. "Don't you like me?"

"Well, you opened up our life together by calling me 'fuck-face' so excuse me if I didn't leap into your arms."

"Is that the way it's going to be?" He asked. "Are you one of those weird bastards that came here to study and better yourself?"

I was being challenged. It was the very first challenge in my college career, and I made what might be the worst choice I'd ever made. As Adam stared me down, I dropped to all fours and fished that can of beer out of the spot where it wedged between the bed and dresser. I flipped the tab open and the beer shot out, but I spilled very little. I placed my mouth over the opening, chugged down the beer, crumpled the can, and tossed it back at Adam. I burped loudly, and returned Adam's piercing stare.

"There you go fuck-wad. You got another one?"

Adam hit me in the center of the chest with my second college beer. We never had a chance.

At precisely noon, a lot of things happened all at once. For one thing a Springsteen alert sounded on my computer. I held my breath, closing my eyes, and hoping that it was the tour announcement. Before I even opened my eyes, however, the ringing telephone in my apartment caused me to jump. I grabbed the portable that I kept next to my bed, and Adam's voice filled my ear.

"Bruuuuuccccceeeeeee! Fuck-face! Bruce is on the move!"

"It's going to be incredible," I said. "Are you one of those weird bastards that isn't going to give up everything in his life and come with us, or are you going to follow the man around and better yourself?"

"I'm in!" Adam said. "The old man has me traveling the country, but I got some vacation time coming. I already told him, when I took the job, that Bruce comes first."

"I bet that went well with your oil tycoon father," I said.

At his age Adam should have probably broken clear of his father's grasp, but it was complicated, and there was about a billion dollars at stake.

"Fuck him. He hates me, but it evens out because I hate him too."

It was the same old Adam. If I was right, his sexual conquests would be discussed next.

"Dude, you should see the broad I was with last night. She was a Swedish chick. I swear to God her nipples were like pencil erasers."

"Anyhow," I said.

"Seriously, she was drop-dead gorgeous and she didn't speak a word of English. I was doing the Swiss Miss commercials to her all night, but I'm telling you, the bitch could drink."

Adam's job for the past two and a half years was to go across the country in advance of the high-powered executives in his father's company. Adam had an unlimited expense account, and his job was to sleep in the best hotels, eat at the best restaurants, attend expensive events, and simply report back to the company about where and when they should book their trip. He was actually quite good at the job, but there had been times when he'd been too drunk to file the one page report he needed to file. He was actually the biggest failure of all of us, but he was in line to inherit what would amount to a cool billion dollars.

"I saw Mary yesterday," I said. "She is in too, and we might have a couple more along for the ride. You know that Mary is going to limit the cash we bring along with us, so don't try and hide anything. We might ask you to get the van we are going to need to travel around in though."

Adam launched into a diatribe about the vehicle that he had the eye on for the job, but as he spoke, my eyes drifted to the computer screen. The first leg of the tour had been introduced, and to my incredible surprise Bruce was starting in the United States. My heart leapt.

"Hey fuck-face, are you listening?" Adam's voice brought me back into the conversation, but only for a moment. I nearly feinted to the floor when I saw the date as I scrolled down:

Buffalo New York, First Niagara Center, May 7, 2012.

I was reading at a frenetic pace. Adam was back to talking about the Swedish girl, and I giggled just to let him know I was interested. Bruce was starting the tour in Cleveland on May 3rd before shuffling off to Buffalo then to Pittsburgh then to Toronto before spending three straight nights at the Meadowlands Complex in New Jersey. From Cleveland through New Jersey our trip would span about two weeks. We would attend seven shows.

"And when I looked up, her ass was right in my face, so I bit it!" Adam said.

"You did not!" I said.

"I swear to God. That's the end of the Swedish chick, I'm afraid."

I thought about sharing the information about the tour with Adam, but I didn't want to bog him down with too many details.

"We need you here in Buffalo by May 1st," I said. "Tell the old man that you won't see him until after Memorial Day."

"Done!" Adam said. "And if Bruce shakes my hand he'll ask me to join the band. I may never have to work again."

Adam laughed at his own joke. He'd never worked a day in his life, and it was exactly what he was trained to do.

"Later, fuck-face. The dogs on Main Street howl."

"Because they understand," I said.

Adam was off the line. I printed out the tour schedule, but not before putting on *The River* and jamming with Bruce and Little Steven through the opening of *Ramrod*. Life just couldn't get much better.

I flopped down on the bed and listened to the music as I daydreamed about finally seeing Bruce face-to-face. I considered an old story about a woman in St. Louis who had waited for Bruce after a show in the 80's and invited him to dinner. Bruce accepted the invitation, made friends with the lady and her family, and stopped by her home every year after the St. Louis show.

"He's just a regular guy," I whispered. "He'll know how much we need him."

I thought of the time when Adam and I had seen Bruce on back-to-back nights in Washington, D.C. on the *Human Touch* tour. Bruce wasn't with the E Street Band for that tour, but the concerts had been great, of course, and Adam and I had slammed a lot of beers. After tailgating for hours in the parking lot Adam had slipped into the woods to take a leak. He weaved his way back into the woods and startled a woman who was also in the woods taking a leak. She screamed, he screamed, and the cops led him away in handcuffs. For Adam it was just another day at the office.

I opened the computer again as Bruce broke into the one song that always made me feel like I could cry, *Wreck on the Highway*. I was singing along with the narrator, matching Bruce note for note when I opened up an email from Anna. After reading it, it wasn't the song that broke my heart and made me cry.

"Hi Joe, I hope you're okay. I had to sneak on. Dad said I can't talk to you no more. He said you're weird. I hate him!!! Can you talk to Mom pleeeeaaaasssse!"

I read the note ten times and the rage surged through my body. As I was reading another email notice filled my box. It was also from Anna. "P.S. please keep sending me letters every day! I love you!"

CHAPTER 5 – FUCKING BUFFALO NEW YORK

The traffic moves infrequently in the middle of a January night in Buffalo. I know because I spend a lot of time, awake, trying to count the cars and imagining where they are all heading. I had spent three days trying to get a hold of Rachael. I continued with my letters to Anna, but other than her 'I hate Dan' note, she did not reach out again. The whole thing was eating me alive, and to be honest, taking a lot away from my planning for the tour.

I glanced at the digits on my cell phone which I kept plugged in at the side of my lonely bed. It was thirteen minutes after two on the morning of January 14. It registered that it was a Saturday, but since losing my job that didn't mean much to me. Every day was virtually the same. I'd chat with Rolando, listen to a Springsteen album, write my note to Anna, listen to a different Springsteen album, and cook, clean, and dream that I was actually living a life.

Realizing that sleep wasn't going to come calling I shrugged off the covers, and headed for the computer. I had a bootleg DVD of the very last Springsteen and the E Street Band performance. It was from November 22, 2009 in 'Fucking' Buffalo, New York as Bruce had called it during his tour. He had talked of meeting Clarence for the first time, and then lapsing into a beautiful dream that took him all over the world and, brought him fortune and fame. He claimed to have been awakened on that very night in November, in Buffalo.

I thought of how I felt when he said that. It seemed as if he was singing straight to me, and little did he know that I had followed every length of his journey. I got the DVD settled into the computer and was just about to hit play when my ringing doorbell sent me to the ceiling. It was so disconcerting that I had to remember if I'd ever heard it ring before. Whoever was outside was leaning on it steadily, and I ran to the side window and tried to see who it was, but I didn't have much of an angle. Instead, I ran to the door and threw it open; about to give holy hell to whomever it was; except I couldn't conjure up even a single sound. Layla was dancing, without a coat, on my front stoop.

"Let me in!" She cried out.

"What the hell are you doing here?"

Layla shrugged by me and into my apartment. She tripped her way through the threshold and the thin yellow shirt she was wearing rode halfway up her back and I glimpsed her tattoo…and her perfect behind.

"I was with Mary! She told me where you lived. You want to party with me?"

I wasn't sure how I was going to break the news that I hadn't partied in a long time, and that my definition of a party these days was mixing hamburger with my mac and cheese.

Layla came straight towards me. She put her frozen hands to my cheeks. "Are my hands cold?"

I could feel that my mouth was hanging open. She leaned in and hugged me.

"You feel so warm. Were you sleeping, Joseph?"

I was wearing a concert shirt from *The Ghost of Tom Joad Tour* over red pajama pants. Layla was in jeans with that low-cut yellow blouse. She must have been absolutely numb from the cold. I headed to my bed and removed the comforter. I was able to hand it back to her because she had followed me like an obedient dog.

"Oh thank you, thank you, thank you! We should have called you tonight. Mary called me to have a couple of drinks with her because asshole Ralph came home drunk and hit her right in the fucking mouth!"

Layla had more than a couple of drinks. I was guessing she'd had about ten.

"Do you have any beer?"

That was a good question. I drank so infrequently that I wasn't even sure. I headed for the kitchen, still waiting for something clever to pop into my head, and Layla followed right behind me.

"You don't mind that I stopped over, do you? Mary kept going on and on about what a great guy you are. Blah, blah, blah, blah fucking blah, and since I ran away from home today, and since I don't have anywhere to go, I hoped you'd let me in."

I glanced in the refrigerator hoping that I wouldn't find a beer. She had moved out of her house? Where would she go?

"My father is a real asshole," she said. "Actually he's not even my real father, but he pretends he is, and I've just had enough, you know? When I saw Mary reading your palm I saw real love and I got to thinking that I needed that in my life, you know?"

Layla sat at the kitchen table. I didn't have any beer, but I took out the half-gallon of milk. I planned on offering her coffee, but I'd lost my ability to speak.

"After I met you guys I went home and my bitch of a mother started in on me. 'When are you going to get a job? Why don't you get off your ass?'"

I filled the coffeemaker and nodded. I was still voiceless.

"Then the old man joined in. I know he's been tapping his secretary for years, and Mom knows it too, for that matter, so when he started harping on me, I brought that little tidbit to the forefront. He called me a 'whore' and one thing led to another, and I stormed out of the house with the clothes on my back."

All at once the drunken façade was replaced with a countenance of true fear. The smiling, obnoxious girl who'd busted through my door only moments before transformed into a slobbering, weeping mess. I dropped to my knees in front of her chair. Still unable to speak I heard Bruce in the background as he droned on about getting through it all on *Lonesome Day*. The aroma of the coffee brewing filled the room. Layla was sobbing gently. I pulled her close, the comforter keeping us apart enough so that it wasn't weird. Her head dropped to my right shoulder.

"You can stay with me," I said.

I can't be sure, but that may have been the precise second when we both felt the love that we were really, truly missing.

The rest of the night was spent drinking pot after pot of coffee. Neither one of us had anything to do the next day, or the day after that, or the day after that, so we talked, and we listened to Bruce.

"He kinda' sucks, you know?" Layla said as we listened to *Mary*

Queen of Arkansas from Bruce's first record.

"This isn't his best effort," I said.

"He mumbles," Layla said. She was lying on my bed, and I was a safe distance away, sitting on the chair in front of my computer.

"I can't really understand him."

For my entire adult life any criticism of Bruce was followed by my staunch defense. I decided to let Bruce defend himself. I put *Badlands* on and turned it up. I decided to sing along so that Layla would get the full punch.

Layla was laughing hard, and I can't imagine why she wouldn't. I wasn't exactly the performer that Bruce is, but I did my best to mimic some of the moves. The coffee was a keen catalyst. Layla's laughter was under control when I got to the high point at the end of the song.

Layla had gained her feet. She met me at the front of the computer where I'd been pacing as if on stage. The lyrics had spoken to her.

"That's awesome," she said. "It sounds like he's talking about me and what's in my heart."

"That's what's in all of our hearts," I said. I turned the volume down a bit as the CD went from *Badlands* to *Adam Raised a Cain*, a song that always made me consider my Dad.

"What about you?" Layla asked. "Did you get along with your parents?"

She was within three feet of me. It was impossible not to feel her physical presence, but her question nearly knocked me off my feet.

"My mom died when I was thirteen," I said. "She had cervical cancer. My Dad put a bullet through his frontal lobe when I was twenty-six."

The room was eerily quiet with Bruce the only voice in the room.

"Oh my God," Layla squealed as the reality of all of it crashed down on her pretty head.

"I don't want to talk about it anymore," I whispered.

Layla stepped close and I stepped away. It was quarter to six in the morning and suddenly I was real tired. I waited for *Adam Raised a Cain* to end as I hate turning Bruce off mid-thought, and I flopped down on the bed. A minute or so later, Layla was beside me, her breath in my ear, as she hugged me close.

"Do you want to 'do me'?" she asked.

"No. Thanks for the offer, but just having you near is perfect," I answered. "I just want you next to me all of a sudden."

We fell asleep like that, two miserable human beings just looking to hang on to something.

"Why is life so fucking hard?" Layla asked just before sleep took control. Those were the last words we spoke that morning. The reason being, of course, was that I didn't have an answer.

Just four hours later, for the second time in just a short time, the thing that made me jump clear to the ceiling was the sound of my ringing doorbell. I turned in the bed and was face-to-face with Layla's pretty, opening eyes. She wore a look of surprise, and for the first time I really noticed how pronounced her dimples were.

"Who's here?" she asked. "Did my stepfather track me down?"

I hadn't thought of that. I imagined that he was about my age. He most likely wouldn't be enamored with my sleeping in the same bed as his child.

I scrambled out of the bed and promptly slammed my big toe off the leg of the bed.

"Fuck!" I grabbed my toe and hopped from the room as the sound of Layla's melodic laugh filled the air. The doorbell sounded again.

Once again opening the door brought an epic surprise. Standing side-by-side were Rolando and Peabody.

"What the hell are you two doing together?" I asked.

"This guy came looking for you," Rolando said. "I told him you were beating your meat in your lonely apartment."

Just then Layla made an appearance and stood at my right shoulder. She leaned in real close. Rolando and Peabody had the exact same reaction to the sight of her; their mouths opened to an O-shape.

"His days of beating his meat are over," Layla said, and she kissed me on the right cheek and headed back into the apartment. It took the two men standing on my stoop a full minute to speak, with Rolando going first.

"When you're done with this douche, come see me. We have to talk!"

If Peabody was offended about being called a douche he didn't show it. Instead he started right in on the reason for his visit. He still looked flustered after seeing Layla, but he tried to be all-business.

"You need to come back to work. The woman is talking lawsuit for your accident and if it comes out that we fired you it might show that we thought it was entirely your fault."

"Which it wasn't," I said.

"I agree," Peabody said. "So, what do you think?"

"I want a raise," I said.

Peabody nearly laughed but he held it in. His face twitched and contorted. I knew that he didn't have any choice in the matter.

"A dollar more an hour," he said.

"Two dollars; take it or leave it."

Peabody's face flushed. I could almost see him doing the math. If he paid me two more dollars an hour I'd be in his pay scale neighborhood.

"I'll let you know when we need you. Also, there's no talking to anyone about the accident. Our lawyers are telling us to stay quiet."

"How's the woman?" I asked.

"Who gives a shit?" Peabody asked. "I'll call."

I was about to head back into the apartment but Rolando was in the center of the gas station parking lot pointing at the center of my chest.

"A little later!" I said. "I'm not quite done in here yet."

I was laughing as I shut the door, but my surprises for the morning weren't over yet. Layla was holding my portable phone out to me.

"Who's Rachael?" she asked.

I hushed Layla and grabbed the phone. The line was dead.

"What did she say?" I asked.

"Nothing," Layla said. "She sounded like a stuck-up bitch though so when she asked me who I was I told her that I was banging you. Was that the wrong thing to do?"

"Oh, God, why would you do that?"

"I live to shock people," Layla said. "If I'm going to move in here, you better get used to that."

What had I got myself into? I couldn't imagine what Rachael was thinking of me now. My life was all about being able to reach out to Anna. I'd have to make it better, and although I was scared, deep down, I was also a little excited about the sudden turns in my life. For the first time since Rachael left, I felt completely alive.

"Do you mind if I shower?" Layla asked.

Before I could even answer she pulled her shirt up over her head and dropped it to the floor. She quickly stepped out of her pants and twirled before beginning a slow walk to the bathroom door.

"I like to shock people," she yelled as the door closed.

Twenty minutes later Layla was lounging on my couch as I wrote my daily note to Anna.

"Hi my little baby girl! I hope that you're in a better mood now. Things are going to be great for you out there in California. Don't worry so much! Life has a way of twisting and turning like a roller coaster and if you hang on tight, relax a little, and smile, you'll enjoy the ride. Our word of the day is *mordant*. Mordant means biting and caustic in thoughts, manner or style. It really isn't good to have a mordant personality because that means you are like a mean person. Remember, it's better to be happy and positive than sad and mordant!

I read something else that you might like. It's a quote by Martin Luther King Jr. I know that you know about him, right? Anyway, he said, *Darkness cannot drive out darkness; only light can do that. Hate cannot drive out hate; only love can do that.*

So, my little baby girl, remember the love! I love you more than anything in this world and my love will help you drive out all of the things that make you sad. Your bonus daddy loves you!"

I hit send on my note just as Layla walked into the room. It dawned on me that she was closer to Anna's age than mine. I had to lay down the law.

"If you're going to stay here, we need a few ground rules," I said.

"Okay," Layla said, "but before you yell at me can you do me a favor?"

"Sure," I said.

"Put some fucking Springsteen on," she said.

That surge that came with being alive blasted through my veins once more.

CHAPTER 6 – WE TAKE CARE OF OUR OWN

Rolando was waiting for me. Layla was absolutely enraptured in an episode of *Jersey Shore* so I escaped to the bitterly cold Buffalo air and made the trek across the parking lot. Rolando was sitting behind the counter working on the morning letter jumbo from the *Buffalo News*.

"It's about fucking time," Rolando said. "Now tell me about that piece of tail."

The fact that he had referred to Layla in such a manner was absolutely disconcerting. In my heart I was already defending her.

"It's not like that," I said.

Rolando was perplexed. I saw his wheels turning. Why would she be in my apartment if it weren't about getting something?

"Are you going to stand there and tell me that the streak is still alive? You still haven't done it?"

"Honest to God," I said. I raised my hand as though I were swearing in at a jury trial. Rolando shook his head in pity.

"I really don't get you, man. Do you mind, then, if I take a poke at her?"

I nearly laughed. I could only imagine how Layla would tear up poor Rolando.

"She's just a kid who's lost her way. I'm trying to help her get things straightened out."

Rolando didn't bother holding back his laugh. He let me have it with both barrels. "You're going to help her? You can't stay out of your own way. I'm a loser, and I feel great when I'm in your presence. Is that how you're going to do it? Are you going to take away her fear of being at rock-bottom by showing her how low a person can truly go?"

I didn't see a way out of the spiral of the conversation so I headed to the coffee maker. "Have you made any changes since the robbery?" I asked.

"What am I gonna' do?" Rolando asked. "Do you think I'm running scared? No one scares the shit out of old Rolando, right?"

I definitely saw fear in Rolando's eyes as they gripped the floor, but I decided to let it pass.

"I did get this though," Rolando said. "It's a nine millimeter. It'll blow a hole right through ya."

I turned away from the task at hand to look at the gun and I ended up spilling milk all over the counter."

"Clean it up, bitch," Rolando said as he pointed the gun at me.

"Yo! Don't point that at me!" I yelled.

"Relax," Rolando said. "The safety is on. It won't be if I ever see that asshole again."

Rolando put the gun back under the counter. I fished in my front pocket for my coffee money.

"Keep it," Rolando said, "but if you get the chance, bring that chick by. Man, her ass was unbelievable. One of us has to get some of that."

I took a sip of coffee. It was bitter and lukewarm; just what I'd gotten used to.

"Say who you like in the bowl?" Rolando asked.

"New England," I said. "Brady is too good."

Rolando howled. "Wrong again," he yelled. "It's all about Manning. I'll bet you fifty that the G-men take them down."

I wasn't exactly sure why I did it. Perhaps it was the need to make everyone in the world appreciate Bruce as I did. God knows it wasn't because I wanted Rolando to be a member of our traveling crew.

"How about this?" I asked. "If New England wins you go on the tour with us to meet Springsteen. If the G-men win, I pay you the fifty."

"Is little piece-o-ass going with you?" Rolando asked.

"Yep."

Rolando extended his beefy hand across the counter.

"You have yourself a deal," he said. "I'll bring my gun too."

I shook Rolando's hand, all the while wondering why the hell I was doing so.

As I made my way across the parking lot a stray quote worked its way through my brain. I considered including it in my daily email to Anna. It was by a fellow named RW Emerson, who according to my quote book said a lot of interesting things. *Always do what you are afraid to do.* I was certainly afraid to bring Rolando into my world, but why not? Now that I was starting to feel alive, why the hell wouldn't I start taking chances?

Twenty minutes later it was readily apparent that the rest of my day was going to be spent taking a huge chance. Layla wanted to head to her parents home to gather up her things so she could officially move in. She met me at the door as I returned from my trip to visit Rolando.

"This place really needs a woman's touch," she said. "I have a bedroom filled with beautiful things. Let's go get 'em. And, by the way, I have a surprise for you."

She headed to the computer and opened up my I-Tunes library. "I have a favorite Bruce song," she said.

I wasn't how sure I was about her touching my things, but I decided to put it out of my mind because, truthfully I was enjoying looking at her from behind as she bent at the waist to find the song she was looking for. The simple fact that she had found a favorite Bruce song was also undeniably exciting as well. She clicked the mouse and the opening chords to the live version of *Out in the Street* blasted through the apartment.

Layla sang the opening line about dressing up pretty. She was wonderfully off-key.

She grabbed my hand and we waltzed our way through the next three verses, with both of us absolutely screaming the chorus about being out in the street where everything promised to be all right..

The end of the song found her just inches from me, our bodies touching; our lips dangerously close to being pressed together. I felt the hunger rising from my toes, but I thought of Anna, and Rachael, and the fact that Layla was just a confused, messed-up girl. We held one another for a moment longer, and Layla won the staring contest that I'm sure she thought would end up in a passionate kiss.

"What sort of trouble are we going to face if we go and get your things," I said. The I-Tunes shuffle took us to *Reason to Believe* from the Nebraska album.

"Oh, the old man will kill you if he sees you," she said. "But he ain't home. He likes to meet up with his whore this time of day, and Mom will most likely be out shopping. I figure we have a good couple of hours to clean out my stuff."

All at once, one of the worst ideas I've ever had entered my brain.

"Do you mind if we bring someone along with us?" I asked.

"What harm would it do?" Layla asked.

***

A half an hour later the three of us were parked in front of Layla's home in the Town of Cheektowaga. Rolando was seated behind the wheel of his grey panel van and I was in the backseat looking out the driver's side window.

"Are we ready for the mission?" Rolando asked.

Layla had just wanted to jump from the car and race to the front door, but Rolando's words of caution had kept her riveted to her seat.

"We have to be stealth-like," Rolando said. "The neighbors will call the cops if we just start loading stuff out the front door, so this is what we're going to do."

Rolando was speaking in hushed tones. I imagine that he was upset that he didn't have time to design a complete separate language so that we wouldn't be detected, but since I saw no harm in allowing him his fantasy, I sat back and listened.

"Joseph is going to climb that pine tree leading to the window on the side of the house. You don't lock the windows on the upper level, do you?"

"No," Layla said.

"Good. Joseph will jump from the tree to the window ledge, prop open the window, come down the stairs and let us in through the back door."

I had just one question.

"Are you out of your fucking mind?" I asked.

Rolando spun in the seat to face me. His expression was a mixture of pain and disbelief.

"Problem?" he asked.

"A couple," I said. "First, that's a jump of about 12 feet. Do I look like Kobe Bryant? Secondly, why can't we just use her key to open the back door and walk in?"

Rolando lowered his head and used his thumb and forefinger to pinch the aggravation out of his eyes.

"Fine!" he said. "We'll do it your way. I'm the best *Tour of Duty* gamer in this town for a reason, but if you know better than me, then fine."

It was around then that I noticed how Rolando was dressed. Up to that point his camouflage pants and the war paint on his face had meant very little to me. He was on a secret mission. It dawned on me that I may have made an error in judgment.

"Hey, Rolando, you don't have that gun on you, do you?"

Layla's eyes were wild with excitement. Rolando offered a sarcastic smile.

"Oh please, please, please shoot my stepfather!" she said.

"Abort the mission!" I yelled.

"*Out in the Street*," Layla requested, and before we left the car we listened to the song on Rolando's stereo.

Thankfully, we used the key and walked straight through the back door to the big, off-white house in the middle of the quiet neighborhood.

It turned out I had worried for nothing. The house was empty, and once inside we were able to quickly gather all of Layla's things. I allowed Rolando a few moments of fantasy as we made zig-zag movements, hiding behind bushes and staying clears of windows and doors. Once more, the feeling that we were living people doing real life things made me feel as if I were one-hundred-percent alive.

Layla was sensible about what she packed for her trip out of her childhood home. We grabbed her laptop, and a few bags of clothes. Although she owned about sixty stuffed animals she grabbed just four or five of her favorites.

The home was peaceful. It was the same sort of home that Rachael, Anna and I had shared. It was a typical, Rockwell painting dream type of home that seemed to convey love between a man, his wife and their child. I felt a twinge of guilt as we gathered one last box for each of us to load into the back of the van.

"Let's trash the place," Rolando said.

"No," I said.

"Yes," Layla answered.

We may have been fortunate that Layla's father's car coming down the street settled the argument for us.

"He's here!" Layla screamed.

I escaped the front door and was to the back of the van before the car screeched to a halt in the driveway. Layla had also made a beeline for the van and was inside and nestled on the floor of the passenger side. It was Rolando who posed the problem.

To be perfectly honest, and in his defense, Rolando most likely hadn't broken into a run in a lot of years. When confronted with the idea of running or walking slowly, directly into the eyes of a confrontation, Rolando certainly had little choice. His extensive *Tour of Duty* experience had fully prepared him for this moment in time.

Layla's father was a big man. From my spot low to the floor in the back of the van I placed him at a shade over six-feet tall and at roughly 220 pounds. He was also quick on his feet, and like a shot was heading straight for Rolando.

"Put the box down," Layla's father yelled. "Layla, get out of that car!"

The man's approach was quickly halted by the sight of Rolando bending low and placing the box on the ground and then rising with the gun high, and pointed to the center of Layla's father's chest.

"On the ground," Rolando bellowed.

"Jesus, no!" I cried out.

"Shoot him!" Layla yelled. "He abused me!"

Layla's father dropped to his knees, never once taking his eyes from the gun. The two men were separated by about twenty feet. Without even thinking about it I slipped into prayer. The words of the *Our Father* were filling up my head. Rolando wouldn't really shoot him, would he? Layla didn't actually want us to murder her stepfather, did she? He had abused her? She had never mentioned the abuse. He had tortured Layla?

Rolando kept the gun trained on the man's head as he called my name.

"Joseph, come and get this box."

Layla was in tears. She turned to face me.

"He abused me," she whispered. "Please. We have to get out of here."

She fumbled with the knob for the stereo and found *Badlands* by accident. The weirdest moment of my life followed as I exited the car, stepped over Layla's stepfather, retrieved the box and listened to Rolando's even tone as he explained how the rest of the adventure would play out.

"I'm going to ask you to stay on the pavement with your face pressed to the ground," Rolando said. "I will have the gun pointed to the back of your head, okay, and if you raise your head, even an inch, it's going to be lights out tonight, forever. Do you understand?"

The man murmured something. I raced to the car, threw the box on the seat beside me, and lowered the window so I could hear the rest of the threat.

"Your days of torturing your lovely daughter are over," Rolando said. "She is with friends now so don't try and stop us and don't come looking for her, because I am a trained assassin and I know exactly where you live."

To his credit, Layla's father didn't move his head at all. Rolando stepped over the top of the man, opened the driver's side door and slid into his spot behind the wheel. He backed out of the driveway as though we were on the way to the mall to catch a movie. There weren't any screeching wheels, or screams of terror.

"He's going to get the license plate number," I worried.

"I don't have plates," Rolando shouted over the sounds of *Badlands* and Layla's sobs. I fell back in the seat as Layla's childhood home disappeared in our rearview mirror.

Six hours later I sat in front of my computer screen. I never really cared for drinking to forget my troubles but there was a glass of Jameson's Irish whiskey at my right hand. Layla was sleeping in my bed, her even breathing offering a rhythmic melody to the fear in my heart. That man had abused her. She told me as much of the story as her heart would allow her to tell, but it had happened more than fifty times over the course of her young life. Deep down, I almost wished that Rolando had shot him. How do people live in such a manner? Why do we hurt each other so? I thought of the fact that I had prayed during the moment of crisis. Was there even a God listening? What would I do to a man who did such a thing to Anna?

I must admit that I was truly in a horrible place as I turned on my computer, but in a world of instant gratification a few things happened real quickly to allow me a bit of hope. I saw two emails beckoning to me. The first was from the Bruce fan site announcing that the single from his new release *Wrecking Ball* was available on I-Tunes. The song was titled, *We Take Care of Our Own*.

The second email was from Rachael. I clicked it open.

"Joseph, don't worry about Dan. Please keep in touch with Anna. Please."

I brought up the new song by Bruce and listened to it through my headphones. Once more, it spoke straight to my heart, but I knew that it would. I read the email about a hundred times as I sipped the Jameson's and watched Layla's eyes flutter as she slept. Her right arm was wrapped around a white, stuffed, bear with red eyes. Layla had a stranglehold on that poor bear. I would take care of her and Anna. My life had sudden purpose.

"Hi, my little baby girl! Have I told you today how much I love you? I don't think that I have! A lot has been happening for me lately, but I want you to know that I will always be here to take care of you. No matter what happens in our lives, I am right here for you because that's the way love is. Love is never hurting the people in your life. Love is about being there through thick and thin and taking care of what is important. I have one thing I want you to remember. It's a quote from a man named R.W. Emerson: *Always do what you are afraid to do.*

Our word of the day is a funny one. It is *weltzchmerz*, and it's a mental depression or apathy caused by the comparison of the actual state of the world with an ideal state. Remember, even when things seem to be at their worst, they can get better, and you shouldn't let it get you down because, Anna, you will always be okay if there are people around who want to take care of you. And I will always take care of you. Your bonus daddy really loves you."

CHAPTER 7 – I TOOK A WRONG TURN AND I JUST KEPT GOING

I'd be lying if I said that the first week with Layla as my roommate was easy. In fact, there were moments when I honestly think it wouldn't work, but I was all-in. It had to work, for both of our sake. So, we fought for every inch of that place, finally figuring out that if I showered in the morning while Layla slept in, we'd be much better off.

Sleeping was another real adjustment. You see, after that first night, when we slept side-by-side without regard to 'doing' her, Layla grew comfortable. We shared the bed. Ass-to-back we slept, like an old married couple. Neither of us worried about it escalating into something uncomfortable. We just needed one another right there, at arm's length.

Layla made good on her promise to clean up the apartment. I was now the proud owner of a few decorative candles, assorted knick-knacks, and bleach that cleaned the disgusting rim around the toilet.

"I hate a dirty bathroom," Layla had said on her first full day in the apartment. "The pubic hair rug had to go."

I returned to my job at Target and my daily meetings with Rolando. Layla cleaned the apartment, cooked perfect dinners, and I'm assuming took long baths and even longer naps. She did her best to shock me with stories of her past, but we steered clear of the truth behind her stepfather's actions. We never heard a word about Rolando's brandishing of a firearm and the man seemed to have let bygones-be-bygones. There were moments, as I watched Layla sleep that I dreamed of shooting the bastard between the eyes. But I let it go. Life was growing comfortable. I should have known better than to imagine that it could stay so peaceful.

On Saturday morning on the twenty-eighth of January I made my way across the parking lot for my morning coffee. The Buffalo winter had been mild up to this point, and it was fairly comfortable this morning. The sun was beginning to climb, and I looked up and around, saying hello to a mother that I hardly knew, and a father that I couldn't save.

"What's up ass-wipe?" Rolando asked as I opened the door. He was studying the daily racing form. "Is your pitiful streak still intact or did the beautiful Layla relent and toss you a pity screw?"

"I'm still the king of my castle," I said.

I followed my daily ritual. Once more the milk container was empty and I retrieved another.

"What time should I be there tonight for the housewarming party?" Rolando asked.

"Uh, what the hell are you talking about?"

"For dinner," Rolando said. "Layla invited me over. Uh-oh, maybe I wasn't supposed to tell you. Perhaps this is her striving for the moment when Rolando finally gives in and teaches her about pure ecstasy."

Rolando waved his hands in front of his massive frame and I laughed. Yet Layla hadn't mentioned a word about dinner, and I wasn't sure that it was the greatest idea in the world.

"Oh, that's right! We'll eat at seven so if you want, come by a little before then."

Once more Rolando waved off my attempt to pay for my coffee.

"I think about her stepfather a lot," Rolando said. "I don't think he should be able to live his life without paying for that."

"Yeah but we have to let it go," I said. "As much as we might want to, we can't right every wrong. She's safe now."

"I *might* let it go," Rolando said.

I paid for the *USA Today* and the *Buffalo News* and headed for the door. The front page of the national paper was home to a story about a triple murder. I pointed to the headline.

"Isn't life grand?" I asked before fist-pumping Rolando and heading back to the parking lot to look once more at the rising sun.

Six hours later I was in aisle number four at Target. I was stocking the shelves behind a movable fence that isolated my work. The store was mostly empty anyway, but Peabody went out of his way, each hour, to remind me that I had to be sure not to cripple any more old ladies.

"JOSEPH, LINE ONE!"

Who the hell would be calling me on the store phone? I pulled my cell phone out of my red apron. I hadn't powered it on. I made my way to the phone in the break room and punched the blinking light beside line one.

"Joseph, You gotta' come home!" Layla was in full scream. I

pictured her pretty face contorted with worry and fear.

"What's wrong?"

"It's Mary. She just showed up all beat to hell. That mother-fucker Ralph kicked the shit out of her. I think he broke her nose."

"Okay, calm down, Layla. Does she need to go to the hospital?"

"She won't," Layla said. "She doesn't want the cops to know. She said she just wants to lie down. We have to let her stay here."

Peabody entered the break room. He absolutely hated when someone took a personal call on 'his' time. He cleared his throat.

I ignored him.

"Of course she can stay," I said. "I'll be home in twenty minutes."

"No you won't," Peabody announced.

"Excuse me a second," I said to Layla, covering the bottom of the phone with my right hand.

"Get the fuck away from me," I said to Peabody.

"Twenty minutes," I said into the phone.

Peabody's face was contorting into his 'I'm the boss' face.

"I have a family emergency," I said as I removed my apron and let it fall to the floor.

"You don't have a family," Peabody said. "Everyone knows you don't have a life." He offered a nervous laugh but his expression went dour when I gave him the finger.

"I'll let you know if I can come in on Monday," I said. "If you dock me I'll be awfully uncooperative regarding that little lawsuit matter."

"At least pick up your apron," Peabody said.

"You pick it up," I said.

I was done being a patsy. It was time to be a man. I hustled to my car in the back lot. I kept thinking about the Bruce lyric about not being a boy, but being a man. It hammered away at the front of my mind all the way home.

***

My broken-down green 1998 Ford Taurus made the trip home in record time. I burst through the front door with my heart pounding hard like the Bruce character in the *Downbound Train* song. I hadn't needed to hurry. Layla had it under control.

Layla and Mary were seated beside one another on the couch. Layla was working on the cuts under Mary's swollen right eye.

"This might sting a little," she said as she applied a washcloth to Mary's face.

Mary didn't react to the cloth on her face, but her eyes filled with tears when she saw me.

"He hammered me good this time," she said. "I suppose I had it coming."

"You didn't have it coming," I said. "No one deserves to be punched in the face."

"I had it coming because I never left him...until today, that is."

I knelt down in front of the couch. Layla continued to dab at Mary's eyes, and she gently wiped away the blood that had dried on the left side of Mary's pretty face. I didn't think Mary's nose was broken, but there was plenty of swelling.

"OH SHIT!" Mary yelled out. Her booming scream caused Layla to fall backwards and she would have fallen to the floor had I not been there to grab her.

"What?" I asked.

"THE TICKETS! The tickets went on sale today!"

"No," I said. "They're on sale on the 28th."

The words had no sooner left my mouth when the realization of the date entered my mind. I scrambled to the computer with Mary and Layla trailing close behind.

"I would've received a notification," I said.

I didn't have to do much more than move the mouse before the announcement blasted across my screen. The proclamation regarding the available tickets was followed by a news story.

40 Years Later, Bruce is Still the Boss!

We all read the article together with our faces separated by no more than 6 inches. The news wasn't good.

Springsteen and the E Street Band announced their most recent tour a little over a month ago and today concert dates in 12 cities resulted in serious problems at the Ticket Master site as the tickets went fast.

"Are you fucking kidding me?" Layla asked. "All the tickets are gone for that old bastard?"

Mary and I each turned to her.

"What is he Barney for adults?" Layla asked. "How do you sell that many seats in that short of time?"

"He's Bruce," Mary said. The fact that she'd been battered by Ralph was all but forgotten as the pain of not getting tickets began to sink in.

"How did you miss the day the tickets went on sale?" Layla asked. "All you ever talk about is that guy, and you missed ticket announcement?"

I pushed the keyboard away from me. I lowered my head into my hands, and the answer to Layla's question swept over me.

"It's because I'm a loser," I said. "I've always screwed up. Day after day, week after week, month after month there's one thing you can count on; Joseph will mess it up."

"We need divine intervention," Mary whispered. "Positive thinking will solve this problem for us. Our faith will be rewarded."

I couldn't control the sarcastic laugh that was building inside me. It was all too ridiculous.

"Are you kidding me?" I asked. "Seriously, Mary, are you *fucking* kidding me? You have a busted face, Layla's life is shot already because a perverted bastard treated her like a playground, and I'm completely alone. My mother died; my father shot his head off, and my little girl is living across the country."

The tears flowed down my cheeks as Mary and Layla watched me in absolute horror.

"We decide that Bruce is going to save us by shaking our hands, and I'm too stupid to get our fucking tickets. How is faith going to save us?"

Mary bowed her head. Despite her unshakeable belief that the universe took care of us all, she had to be ready to give up as well. She just had to be.

"Joseph, Joseph, Joseph, I taught you better than that," Mary said. Her voice was soothing. Despite the pain caused by her physical beat-down, she was fully alive inside her wonderful soul.

"I know you so well," she said. "I know how beautiful you really are. What is the one thing you want out of life, Joseph?"

I was up and moving. I kicked the shelf that held my keyboard and Layla had to scramble clear of its descent to the floor.

"I just want to live!" I screamed. "I want a life that's fair. I want to receive a tenth of the love that I give out. I want to arrive in a place where things are settled in my mind. Nothing will ever be settled. They will lower me to the ground and announce that my entire life was unfulfilled. I'm a loser. Is that enough for you? I took a wrong turn and I just kept going, and I'm sick of heading down this loser path."

The spit was flying from my mouth. I thought of Layla being terrified of her stepfather as his huge hands groped her innocent body. I considered that I was scaring her, and even in the midst of my lowest point, I felt badly for someone else.

"Are you done?" Mary asked.

My heart was pounding. We weren't going on the tour. We didn't have a single ticket for even one city. Meeting Bruce wasn't going to save me. There wasn't a single thing that could ever save me. I thought of Rolando's gun. I could borrow it, and the police would confiscate it after I used it to do to me what my father had done to himself. All of these years of blaming him for leaving me, and as it turned out, he was the brilliant one.

His pain was gone.

I fell back on the bed. Neither Layla nor Mary approached me, but when Mary cleared her throat I understood that she'd soon be filling my head with her bullshit theories of peace and understanding.

"As Mother Teresa said, *the success of love is in the loving, it's not in the result of the loving,*" she said. "You are alive because you have love, Joseph. You have more love inside you than you know what to do with."

It was the same sort of shit that I was trying to feed Anna, and who knew what was going on in her life. Maybe Dan was torturing her. Perhaps she would do no better than the rest of us when it came to warding off the horror of the world.

"She's right, you know," Layla whispered. "All we can do is to keep trying. Bruce will come back around again."

It was the very last thing I wanted to hear. I thought of Rachael and how she never truly loved me. She had allowed me to take her in and pretend to be her man because of Anna, but we were never a couple. I had never reached her, despite my golden heart of love. In the end, she discarded me as though I were loose change in her pocket. Rachael had taught me an important lesson. Even though I'd given her everything, it wasn't what she needed. I had walked softly though the world with my head held high and my heart singing the right songs, but I was surrounded by nothing but fog and shadows. Bruce was wrong. Faith, hope and love wouldn't win out.

"Remember what I told you on the day your father shot himself?" Mary asked.

If there was one person in the world that could talk me down off the ledge it was Mary, and the tone of her voice expressed that it was exactly what she intended to do. For good measure, Layla was right beside me too, with her hand on the bare skin of my right arm.

"Do you remember?" Mary whispered.

"Was it the Japanese proverb?" I asked. *Fall down seven times; Get up eight?* I asked.

"No," Mary said. "The other thing I told you. Do you remember that?"

My eyes were closed tightly. Tears were emerging from underneath my pressed lids. Still, Layla's soft hand was running up and down my forearm. I understood Mary's love, but why did Layla love me?

"Think," Mary whispered. "Who is my favorite thinker of all-time?"

"Buddha," I said. "*The mind is everything. What you think you become.*"

"Exactly," Mary said. "Visualize yourself at the concert in Buffalo. Keep your eyes closed, and capture it in your mind. The pre-concert music is playing softly. People are hustling to their seats with their new concert shirts on. The lights go dark. On the stage you see the band coming up the steps. Think of Steven and Patty heading to their spots. Can you see it?"

I nodded, but I thought of the fact that Clarence wouldn't be making the approach. Layla's hand was moving up and down at a more hurried pace. Just the touch of Layla was calming me. Mary's voice was a little different because of her swollen nose, but it was the same beautiful voice I'd heard for years.

"Do you see Bruce yet?" Mary asked. "I know you're looking for him in the dark. Your heart is racing. I'm right beside you, holding your hand as we jump to our feet as he bounds up the stairs. Do you see him?"

"Yes," I whispered.

"You will be there, and you will have a great seat."

Layla's hand moved to the side of my face and she wiped a tear away. My eyes were still closed. My mind was far away, in the crowded arena. I heard Mary moving in my shithole apartment, but that didn't matter right now.

"*Good evening, Buffalo,*" Bruce says. You've heard him say that, right?"

I felt Layla's soft lips on my right cheek as she kissed the spot where my tears had landed. All at once a wall of sound blasted my eyes wide open as the opening chords of the new song blasted through my computer speakers.

"We Take Care of Our Own," Mary shouted as though she were beside me in that seat in the arena. "It's the first song."

As Bruce's voice filled my room, I sat up.

But how would we make it work?

Suddenly Layla scrambled up and off the bed. She raced to the knob of my speakers and turned down the volume. At the very same time both Mary and I yelled at her.

"You can't turn down Bruce!"

"The phone is ringing," Layla said.

I thought of Rachael, or Anna, or Peabody calling me on the house phone, but it was none of the three.

"Hey fuck face," Adam cried out. "Five tickets in the lower level for seven shows. I got 'em, buddy. You said you had two others coming along, right?"

I turned to Mary. She couldn't hear Adam's words in my ear, but somehow she already knew.

"Adam got the tickets," I said. "He got enough tickets for all of us."

I dropped to my knees right there on the floor of my bedroom. Bruce was singing, asking the question about when love would rain over him.

At that very moment, I had an answer for him. I held Mary and Layla for a long moment after getting off the phone with Adam.

"We are having Rolando over for dinner," Layla said. "Mary, let's get to work."

Both of my beautiful women kissed me.

Once more, life had turned on a dime.

"Get some rest," Mary said. "We're going to cook. Her face was battered, but there wasn't a single thing strong enough to stop her. She would take every punch and turn and turn until she found love.

Mary placed her arm around Layla's shoulder, and they actually skipped out of my room.

After a few minutes of peace I headed for the computer.

"To my little baby girl! Oh how I love you! I would count the ways but I can't count that high! I am everywhere when it comes to loving you.

Our word of the day is *ubiquitous*. It means being or seeming to be everywhere or in all places at the same time. I'll use it in a sentence for you. My love for Anna is ubiquitous. My love for you, Anna, is there in the smile that you see on other people's faces. It's in the darkness that surrounds you as you fall asleep at night. Ubiquitous!

Do you remember Ralph Waldo Emerson, baby girl? He said; *Do not go where the path may lead, go instead where there is no path and leave a trail.*"

My love is deeper than all of the oceans combined!"

I clicked send on the email. In the kitchen I could hear the pots and pans being bandied about. We had our tickets to see Bruce. It didn't mean the world was going to spin perfectly, but it was a start.

I thought of Rolando sitting across from me at the dinner table, and I laughed. It was another slow-building laugh that grew into a crying jag.

We had our tickets. It was time to roll down the windows and let the wind blow back out hair.

CHAPTER 8 – THE DOOR'S OPEN BUT THE RIDE AIN'T FREE

I had been banned from the kitchen. Mary delivered a glass of ice water and broke the news to me.

"We have a lot of work to do. We can't have you getting in the way."

So I dialed up *Lucky Town* on my computer and as *My Beautiful Reward* played I scanned my email. Adam sent a recap of our seating arrangements for all of the shows. We were in the first level close to the stage in all cities. For the Pittsburgh show we were a mere twenty rows from the stage. My mind was a whirlwind as I imagined Bruce seeing me from his spot on the stage and waving me to join him in song. I could sing along with *Waitin' on a Sunny Day*. The media would pick up on my rich voice and before long, I'd be writing my own songs and filling arenas with my own band.

I might have stayed stuck in that daydream but as I read Adam's e-mail another message popped into my inbox. It was from Anna.

"Hey, Joseph! How are you? Me and Mom went to Disney. The one in California. It was fun. Dan didn't come with us because he fights a lot with Mom. We both hate it here, but Disney was fun. I went on a ton of rides. You should come and visit sometime. I've been writing down all the words of the day you send me. My favorite word of the day was love. I know what that means because of you. Bye for now."

The say that there is no such thing as a truly broken heart, but I beg to differ. I read an article that the heart cannot physically break. As I reread that note, over and over, it felt as if my heart broke into a million little pieces. The ringing doorbell snapped me back to the living.

"Joseph, get the door," Layla called out.

I heard the sound of the mixer as I ducked by the kitchen and headed for the front door. The fact that my doorbell had rang three times in the past few days was not lost on me. I was spending time with real, breathing people. I swung the door open to find Rolando on the stoop.

"Let me the fuck in," he said. "I'm freezing my ass off out here."

I hadn't been quite prepared for a showered and seemingly clean Rolando. He was wearing an off-white dress shirt with a bright blue tie. I had never actually seen him with long pants on, and I was too stunned to speak, or even allow him the room to pass. In his right hand he held a bouquet of flowers. His left hand was home to a half a bag of potato sticks. He pushed me out of his way.

"Come on, asshole, I'm cold," he said.

I backpedaled into the apartment.

"Stop undressing me with your eyes," he said. "Get those flowers into some water. Let's get a drink."

"Potato sticks?" I asked.

"They're awesome with beer," he said. "You better have some beer."

Layla hugged Rolando hello and the absurdity off it all left me standing there with my mouth wide open. Mary was mashing the potatoes and singing the theme from the *Golden Girls* television show. Layla took two glass mugs out of the freezer and made a major production out of pouring beer into the mugs. Rolando never took his eyes off her backside.

"Men into the living room," Mary said. "We aren't quite ready to serve you yet."

I followed Rolando to the seat in front of the television. He raised his mug in a salute and we clanked glasses. The first sip of the ice cold beer was heavenly.

"To love," he said. He pointed at Layla and mouthed the words, 'she's mine.'

"We got you a ticket to all the Bruce shows," I said.

"Doesn't that depend on who wins the Super Bowl tomorrow?" Rolando asked.

I had forgotten about our bet.

"Just fucking with you," Rolando said. "I'll go. What the hell else do I have to do? They heard about the gun behind the counter and they're deciding if they want to fire me from my shit-ass job."

Rolando drained his entire beer in one gulp, let out a loud belch and called to Layla for a refill. She shook and shimmied her way into the room and refilled his glass, flirting with her eyes as she did so. A moment later she was gone and we watched her leave.

"She's so beautiful," Rolando said. "Maybe she's my reward for having paid the price all these years."

I took my second small sip from the glass.

"What?" I asked.

"Everybody pays to play," Rolando said. "No matter how much we want things to go smoothly, we have to get our fucking teeth bashed in just for the sake of being alive. You should know that better than me. People have been shitting on your head forever, but if you wait around long enough, the gods toss you a piece of primo ass or an iced cold beer to keep you interested."

I laughed. It was the most screwed up thing I'd ever heard.

"Dinner's served," Mary sang out. "Where are our men?"

Rolando drained his second beer. He smoothed his tie, slicked back his hair with a healthy dollop of his own spit, and put his arm across my shoulder.

"Let's go, boy. It's time for a bit of my beautiful reward."

I turned to him in shock.

"Last song on the *Lucky Town* CD," he said. "I've been studying up. He sucks ass, by the way."

The table was something straight out of Martha Stewart's kitchen. The turkey had been expertly positioned as the centerpiece. I wasn't sure where all of the bowls had come from but there were plenty, and they were filled with perfection. There were buttered rolls, cranberries, steamed asparagus, mashed potatoes and homemade stuffing.

"Holy fuck," Rolando said. "I ain't seen a meal like this, ever."

He held his empty beer mug out to Layla. She took it from his hand, rinsed it, and placed it back into the freezer. She removed another frosty mug and poured his beer into it.

"Sit, sit," Mary said. "Time to dig in, but I will be saying a prayer, of course."

I sat across from Mary. It was impossible not to be drawn to her battered face, but the bruises seemed to be fading already.

"God we thank you for the chance to sit down and share this meal," she softly said. "We are a weathered bunch, who doesn't deserve your eternal love, but we want to work hard to find some peace in this mixed-up world and we beg you for your mercy."

Rolando cleared his throat.

"Amen, bitch," he yelled out.

Having known Mary for over twenty years I was sure that she wouldn't take kindly to such an abrupt end to her prayer of thanksgiving, but she simply laughed.

I thought of the dog in the Born in the USA song. The one who ended up so beat up that it spent the rest of its life covering up.

We ate the meal as if our lives depended on it. I couldn't help but marvel about the talents of Layla, and she basked in our praise.

"I cooked every dinner for mom and that pervert," she said. "I only did it for mom, but he never once told me that I'd done well. He had too many secrets."

Another Bruce lyric worked its way through my excited brain as I considered Layla and her sad life up to now. I thought of the woman in the Price You Pay who dreams of living a better world but ends up downhearted as she waits to see some sun. Would that day ever come for any of us?

"*The time is always right to do what is right*," Mary said as she raised her glass in a toast. "Martin Luther King Jr.," she added.

"I hate that fucking guy," Rolando said. "But I got something as long as we are waxing poetic. It's all about honor."

Rolando held his glass out across the table and we all clanked his mug.

"*Get on her and stay on her*," he said. He looked directly at Layla and winked. She was in mid-sip and she spit her beer across the table, directly into Rolando's face.

"That's an old one," Layla said, "but when he winked at me, I lost it."

It was my turn.

"*Blow away the dreams that break your heart*," I said as I raised my glass.

"*Life's a bitch and then you die*," Layla said as we toasted for the fourth time.

As we ate we discussed the plans for the tour. Mary was adamant about the amount of cash we'd each be allowed to bring. She was thinking that our trip should have a Woodstock quality to it and we romanticized along with her. We would sleep in campgrounds around a fire pit. We'd drink a few beers and live, laugh and share.

"I'll bring the dope," Rolando said. "And my gun, of course."

The idea of there being a gun along for the trip turned Mary three shades of red but I shushed her with a finger to my nose. I would handle getting the gun away from Rolando.

Most of my dining experience was spent in awe of Layla. As I watched her eat all I considered was that she was spun from pure gold. Every single movement she made drew my eyes to her and when she smiled it occurred to me that her smile was a lot like what I imagined heaven to be like. I wasn't the only guy at the table falling in love. Rolando was wiping the corners of his mouth with a folded napkin, smiling as though he were a game show host, and working overtime to tell stories that placed him front and center. We ate nearly everything on the table.

"Life is good," I said as I pushed back away from the table. "The men are going to do the dishes."

"The fuck we are," Rolando said.

***

I had insisted. I washed and Rolando dried. He smoked a joint and went on a long dissertation about how awful Springsteen was as both a singer and performer.

"He dances like a white boy and sings like his mouth is filled with marbles."

"Wait until you see him," I said.

"I'm just going along for the tail in that room. Did you see how Layla looks at me?"

Rolando had loosened his tie. He let a blast of gas go and coughed as he did so to muffle the sound.

"I'm only going to tell you this once," I said as I waved my hand in front of my nose. "Layla will handle you the way she wants. If you give her a hard time, I'll defend her."

Rolando laughed so boisterously that he had to sit down. "You're going to defend her honor?" He slapped his knee. "That's hysterical. You were a straight-up stooge for eight years living and taking care of a woman that couldn't stand the sight of you and then you let a man walk right through your front door and take her away. You're like the lion in the Wizard of Oz."

Rolando was on his feet. He moved to within an inch of my face.

"Don't try and be courageous with me," he said. "Cause I ain't stable."

I felt absolute rage building inside me. Rolando was doing his very best to stare me down, but if it was courage that I needed to turn my life around, I was going to start showing it. I stared right back. I would fight him if I had to. I wanted to show him that much. He raised his hand suddenly and I flinched. Rolando smoothed the hair on the right side of his head as he laughed.

"My soft little kitten, Joseph," he said. "We need this trip. I'm going to make a man out of you and Layla is going to show me love."

Rolando draped his arm around my back.

"I hear what you're saying," he whispered. "I know what her step daddy did to her. I will treat her like an angel."

The after dinner party was straight out of the Mary handbook. She lit at least thirty scented candles and placed them strategically around the living room. The candle light was the only illumination, and there was also burning incense that aggravated the piss out of Rolando.

"It smells like a whorehouse in here," were his exact words.

Mary was also in charge of the tunes so there was a heavy emphasis on *The Ghost of Tom Joad* and *Nebraska* records. She introduced Layla and Rolando to the brilliant lyrics of each album, but there were certainly moments when I felt as if we were losing our guests, but Mary was on top of the parlor games as well.

"Biggest regret," she announced. "We're all going to present our cases here. Life is about connecting and holding each other's souls. I know a lot about Joseph, but I want everyone to be totally honest here. The only way to true enlightenment is to communicate. Who's first?"

The room was deathly silent. We all had a drink in our hands and Rolando and Layla were sharing a fat joint. I wasn't much of a drinker but I was even less of a pot-smoker. The fact that I was eternally boring was one of the main grievances Rachael had with me. When her name popped into my head it came out of my mouth.

"Rachael was my biggest regret," I said.

Bruce was singing of *Dry Lightning* and how no one actually gives another exactly what is needed.

"Tell us the story," Layla said. She was sitting between Rolando and me. Her left hand never left my thigh. I knew that was absolutely killing Rolando, but he was behaving so far.

"I knew Rachael back in high school," I said. "Back then she was the prettiest cheerleader. She was whip smart, and was voted the most likely to succeed. But she always had this thing for the worst kinds of guys. She went out with one loser after another. I wanted her so badly, but I was the friend, you know?"

"Geez' there's a shocker," Rolando said. "She probably thought you were a homo."

I ignored Rolando. I hadn't spoken much about Rachael and the pain it caused me. I took a long swig of beer.

"She got mixed up with Dan about twelve years ago, and at first, I thought he'd be different for her. He was successful, well-dressed, and seemed to treat her okay. It saddened me, of course, because I wanted her for myself, but if she was going to be happy."

"Joseph is the best guy in the world," Mary said.

"He just *might* be gay," Rolando chimed in.

"Dan knocked Rachael up, and he just couldn't get away fast enough. I was living alone in a place a lot like this dump. She was sad and lonely. She needed a father for Anna. It certainly seemed like a good idea."

I let the quiet take control of the room. Rolando filled the gap with a loud burp that resulted in a fit of laughter.

"Even your regrets are boring," he said.

"What about you?" I asked. "Why are you so fucked up?"

Rolando didn't answer. Mary saved him anyway.

"You got Anna out of your relationship with Rachael," she said. "That can't be your biggest regret."

"Do you see Anna here?" I asked.

"Granted," Mary said. "But your father shot his head off. I know that bothers you too."

Layla's hand was working overtime on my leg. She was getting dangerously close to the inside of my thigh. God how I loved her.

"This isn't going to be a Joseph pity party," I said. "My Dad lived a tough life. He quit when he lost Mom. I tried my best to make it work, and it didn't."

"You quit school because of his depression," Mary said. "You're much too smart to be stocking shelves at Target."

I waved Mary off.

"Move on, I'm done," I said.

"I'll go," Layla said. She jumped to her feet, and dropped her pants to her knees. Her perfect bottom was just inches from my face.

"This tattoo!" she said. "It's my number one regret. Read it, Joseph."

"I'll read it," Rolando said. He reached out to pinch Layla's ass and she jumped out of the way.

"It says 'I love Toad,'" I said. The light wasn't great.

"Todd!" Layla shrieked as she pulled her pants up. "Todd was my first boyfriend. He was a fucking asshole and now I have this tattoo and it'll be there forever."

"Can I see it again?" Rolando asked. He took a long hit on the joint and coughed his way to another laugh.

"My step-father started coming into my room when I was about eleven," Layla said. Her voice broke and I knew that the tears were coming quickly.

"He told me that I was his girlfriend. When you're that young it gets confusing. My own father had left me. He was doing strange things to me, but he was there, you know?"

"I'm going to kill that man with my bare hands," Rolando said.

"You can't kill what he did to me," Layla said as tears muddled up what she said.

"Real love can kill it," Mary said. "That's what we are here for. That's what this trip will do."

I put my arm around Layla's shoulder and she slipped into me, placing her head on my shoulder.

"Why the fuck are we doing this?" Rolando yelled. "Turn that marble-mouthed mother-fucker off and that's enough with the regret bullshit."

Rolando was on his feet, waving his beer bottle in the direction of the computer where Bruce sang of violence and murder in *Johnny 99*.

Bruce sang about Ralph losing his job at the auto plant and just spinning into a world of violence. The mention of 'Ralph' brought us to Mary.

"Tell us about Ralph," I said as a direct challenge to Mary.

"Yeah, why the fuck do you let some asshole kick the shit out of you every three days?" Rolando was getting dangerously close to belligerent. Layla noticed as well. She offered her hand and Rolando took it, sitting back beside her as he did so.

"Ralph has demons," Mary said. "There are days when he controls them, and he's a solid man. There are days when Satan wins. For the longest time, I felt as if I could help him through the pain. He showed me a lot of physical pain, through the years, but it's the mental beat-down that will be his undoing."

"Oh no," Rolando said. "He's going to get a physical beat-down too. I'm going to kick his teeth down his fucking throat if I ever see him."

"That wouldn't solve a thing," Mary said. "I won't go back to him again, but part of me will always love him."

Rolando brushed Layla off his arm. He found his feet once more, and in the backdrop of *Johnny 99*, Rolando promised true violence against the world.

"You want my biggest regret?" He asked. "Okay, you're going to get it."

Our heads were bowed. Rolando was prancing around the living room with a beer in his right hand. He looked like a demented preacher.

"FUCKING LOOK AT ME!" he shouted. "Look right at me!"

I raised my head slowly.

"I'm a disgusting fat fuck. And do you know what I was before I became a fat fucking, disgusting man? I was a fat, fucking disgusting kid. The guys made fun of me, and the girls looked at me with pity. We were poor. I couldn't buy new clothes. I couldn't lose weight because my waste of a mother stuffed my face with potato chips and cupcakes for dinner. My old man was in jail. For my entire childhood, the mother-fucker was in jail."

There wasn't another sound in the room except for Rolando screaming and Bruce singing softly behind him. The burning incense left a cloud of despair hovering above the coffee table.

"If its love you're offering on this trip to follow old marble-mouth, I'll fucking take it," Rolando concluded. "I'll fucking take it."

He fell back on the couch.

"The dogs on Main Street howl," he said.

"Because they understand," I finished.

We clanked beer bottles.

Yet I wasn't going to let the party end in such a manner.

"That's enough of the despair," I said. "Bruce can take you higher too."

I ran around the room with Layla right on my heels. We blew out the candles and I flipped on the overhead light. I found what I was looking for on the I-pod connected to the computer and the opening chords of *Glory Days* filled the air.

I was on top of the coffee table in the center of the room. The beer fueled my singing voice. My backing vocals screamed out the chorus: *Glory Days!*

The sing-a-long continued straight on through to *Dancing in the Dark.* When I sang the verse about wanting to change my clothes, my hair, my face, Rolando was right beside me.

"This is a good one," he yelled in my right ear. "Let's change everything."

By the end of the song Rolando was shouting in full voice about how his gun was for hire.

I could only hope that he didn't mean it in the most literal of terms. Pain has a funny way of showing itself. Still we were together. A ragtag bag of smashed assholes as Rolando called us. All we needed was Adam and the thin white line of the highway. We were on our way. No one would win unless everyone won.

"I love you," Layla whispered in my ear as we drifted to sleep. Once more, we were side-by-side with Rolando sleeping on the floor of the bedroom, and Mary safely tucked away in the living room.

"We really need love," she said as she closed her eyes on a truly wonderful day.

Chapter 9 – May 1 – 2012 – As Relentless as the Rain

Adam's plane was scheduled to touch the ground at the Buffalo airport at two-thirty in the afternoon. We would have more than two days to get to Cleveland from Buffalo for the first Bruce show, and despite the fact that we were less than three hours, door-to-door we were most likely pushing the envelope. I say all of that because our assembled traveling crew was a tad high-maintenance.

Layla and Mary had shared my apartment all through February, March and April. Despite the fact that we had found our niche in regard to sleeping arrangements, we had certainly run into more than a few complications. For one, Rolando was at the apartment constantly throughout those months. His lust for Layla had transformed into genuine feelings of love, I'm afraid, but there was a part of my brain that figured out he was also in deep love with Mary. Layla, on the other hand, was becoming another extension of my body. She was hanging close to me every minute of the day. We slept side-by-side, but we did not cross the line. I can't say that the thought of making love to her ever escaped my mind, but what Layla needed more than anything else was real love, unconditional trust, and true respect. She wouldn't quite get that from Rolando, but she certainly got it from me.

As we headed toward the airport in the early afternoon Layla was in the passenger seat of my car. Mary with her dangling bracelets and blue and red hair was in the backseat hanging in the space in between me and Layla.

"Why isn't Rolando coming?" Layla asked for the third time.

"He said he's got 'fucking shit' to do before we start chasing 'marble-mouth'," I said.

"Do you think he's going to cause trouble on the trip?" Mary asked. "I love him and everything, but this is a spiritual journey for us. I'm not sure it will be for him."

I merged onto I-90. Layla's hand was intertwined with mine. We always seemed to be holding hands, and I loved it.

"To answer your questions," I said. "First, he's going to cause a lot of trouble, and secondly, Rolando has never been on a spiritual journey in his life."

Layla laughed, but I glanced at Mary's face in the rearview mirror and her forehead was furrowed with lines of worry.

"So we leave tomorrow morning for Cleveland. After that show we are going to head home, right, to save money?"

"Yes," I said. "We'll spend the day before in the city, and travel after the shows. We have enough drivers to make it smooth. We'll sleep in the truck or at campsites."

"You told Adam not to bring thirty-thousand dollars, right?" Layla asked. "Money is the first enemy of spirituality if you ask me."

"The love of money," I said. "That's the real problem."

"You see how it's ruined Adam's life," Mary said.

"Wouldn't ruin mine," Layla said. "What's Adam look like? Maybe I can bag him and live myself a life of leisure."

Layla may have been joking but to be honest, it was one of my biggest fears of the trip. Adam was certainly not above making a play for Layla. If he did, it would rip my heart out because she would probably go for it.

"Trust me," Mary said. "Adam is a dream to look at, but he's a nightmare to love."

Traffic was heavy for the middle afternoon and my car was sputtering along on its last legs. The best part of the entire car was the stereo. I turned up *Out in the Street*, and Layla sang along at full voice. It had turned out to be our song.

"Did you know that Bruce almost didn't put this on *The River*," I said. "He thought it was too idealistic."

"Who gives a shit?" Layla said. "Can't you just listen and enjoy without thinking everything through?"

I supposed that I couldn't. We pulled up to the short-term parking lot, and exited the car. We were hand-in-hand following our spiritual leader, Mary, through the parking lot. For some reason, I had a real sneaking feeling that something bad was about to happen. Things were just too perfect.

Ten minutes later we watched through the window as Adam's plane arrived. We went through the hassle of security so that we could greet him at the gate. Despite the fact that security put Layla through the X-ray where they may or may not see you naked, we got through without any hassles.

Of course, Adam was the first one off the plane. He lived his life in first-class and he wouldn't have had it any other way.

"Oh my," Layla said when I pointed out Adam. Her hand slipped from mine.

Despite the fact that Adam was six months older than me there was no way of guessing such a thing. He still looked as if he were in his mid-twenties. His dark wavy hair was worn long, to his collar. There hadn't been any receding from the front either. Adam had always worked out religiously, constantly bragging to me about the weight he could pump up and over his head. Judging by the size of his arms, he hadn't stopped working out either. He wore a bright red Nike muscle shirt and loose-fitting black jeans. He spotted me looking him over.

"Fuck-face!" he yelled out and thirty people turned to see where he was looking. I tried to be smooth in my approach, but he rushed to me and greeted me with a full bear hug that lifted me from his feet. He put me down quickly when he saw Layla at my side.

"Whoa! What the fuck? You're Layla?"

"Guilty," Layla said. She was blushing from head-to-toe and was kicking at the ground in an awe-shucks sort of pose. Mary was beside me waiting for her hug, but all of Adam's attention had been captured.

"I gotta' tell you." Adam said. "When fuck-face told me he was hanging with a beautiful young girl I was skeptical. He doesn't have much of a track record, other than Rachael, of course, but MY GOD!!!"

Layla twirled for Adam and he whistled. His Nike gym bag was slung over his shoulder. He set it at his feet. "Come and give me a hug," he said, and all of my worst fears came to be. Layla seemed to drop into his arms.

"Hey lover boy," Mary said. "Did you forget about me?"

Adam and Layla broke their embrace but you can't convince me that either one wanted to. Mary replaced Layla in Adam's massive arms. I picked up his gym bag.

"You're traveling light, that's good," Mary said.

"Don't get excited, I checked a bag," Adam said. "I know you like to live like a gypsy but I need to look good. I need clothes to pull it off, ain't I right, Layla?"

"Whatever you're doing keep doing it," Layla said. "Fuck-face tells me you're a millionaire too."

"Billionaire with a 'B'," Adam said. "I'm a billionaire in training."

And there it was. Five minutes after meeting Adam, Layla was calling me 'fuck-face'. Yet as we headed for the baggage claim area a strange thing happened. Mary and Adam took the lead and Layla dropped back and grabbed hold of my hand.

"Sorry about the fuck-face thing," she whispered.

"It's all right," I said. "I know who you really love."

Layla didn't answer me. It seemed to me that she was lost in thought. She was staring straight at Adam's muscular ass.

As we watched the luggage being loaded onto the belt Adam fished the tickets out of his gym bag. He held them up for inspection. We had five tickets for seven shows. Adam did a little dance as he sang the words to *Born in the USA*. He may have gotten three out of ten words right. Of course, his bag was the first one to hit the carousel.

An hour later we were seated around my kitchen table. We all had a beer open and the *Born in the USA* album was playing. Like most educated Springsteen fans I considered *Born in the USA* to have way too many pop songs, but it was Adam's favorite by far. He was trying to sing along with *No Surrender*.

"They don't make them like this anymore," Adam said. He took a slug of his Heineken. "Even Bruce's new stuff doesn't measure up."

"Of course it does," I said. "Have you heard the new album?"

"Not yet. Actually, I have a bone to pick with Bruce. When we meet him I'm gonna' ask him why he's still whining about the poor and downtrodden. He's got more money than my old man. His man-of-the-people act is wearing a little thin."

I sat back as though I had been slapped.

"It's Bruce!" I said. "He's the same as he's ever been!"

Adam laughed.

"Joseph is right," Mary said. "Don't be putting Bruce down. His heart is pure."

Right on cue, *My Hometown* started and a quiet settled around the room as we listened to Bruce sing of looking for work.

"Seriously, he almost lost me there when he was out running around with Obama. Why doesn't he just keep playing the guitar instead of trying to become a political figure?"

Mary took control of the situation.

"We will have no more of that talk," she said. "Springsteen writes about the pulse of the country. It's his job to speak up. Do you think the money and fame has changed him?"

"Money changes everyone," Adam said. "The only people who sing out about despair are the ones who don't have money. People need to get up off their asses and go get some. Success doesn't come to you, you go get it. Am I right, Layla?"

Layla nodded in agreement. Adam patted his lap and Layla would have sat in it if the telephone hadn't rung. Layla, it seems, had a gift for hearing the phone. She turned the stereo down and picked up the portable.

"Calm down!" she said. "She's right here."

Layla handed the telephone to Mary and went to the refrigerator to get Adam another beer. He hadn't even asked for one.

"Oh my God," Mary said. "Is he going to be all right? Where did they take him?"

I moved closer to my old friend. She placed her right hand on her head.

"What?" I asked.

"No," Mary said. "I don't think it's a good idea." The tears started to race down both sides of her face.

"Okay, keep me in the loop. I'll be praying with all of my strength."

Mary let the phone just drop from her hand. It clanked across the table. Adam shrugged. I shrugged, and we waited for Mary to compose herself. Layla was frozen in her spot by the refrigerator, both of her hands wrapped around the green beer bottle.

"They found Ralph in an alleyway," she said. "Someone beat him half to death and stole his wallet. He's in bad shape."

I could still hear Bruce's voice on low in the background. *Born in the USA* had shifted to *Devils and Dust*. I recognized the song as *Long Time Coming*. The irony wasn't lost on me.

"Are you fucking kidding me?" Adam asked. "I wish it was more than half-to-death to be honest. Jesus, Mary he had it coming to him, don't you think? I wish I'd done it myself!"

That was when it hit me.

Where was Rolando?

***

I didn't voice my concerns to anyone. Instead, when Rolando rang the doorbell, I made sure I was the one to answer it.

"Let me in!" he yelled as I approached.

I swung the door open knowing that my fears had been justified. Rolando was sweating profusely and his hair was stuck to his forehead. His right hand was at his side and he shook his fist, as though he were trying to shake away pain. There was blood all over his knuckles.

"Come on!" he said.

"You can't go in there," I said. "Not like that. Mary is really upset."

"Oh, fuck that," he said.

"Who's working the store?" I asked.

The cold air was doing a number on me as I hadn't grabbed a jacket.

"The Chinese dude," he said.

"Will he let you wash up over there?"

Rolando was completely exasperated. He kept looking to the street as though he expected a cop to pull up at any moment.

"Let's go," he said.

At the sink in the backroom of the gas station Rolando filled me in.

"I'd been thinking about it for weeks," he said. "Neither of those guys deserved to go unpunished, so I punished them."

The blood from his knuckles was washing down the sink. Most of the blood hadn't belonged to Rolando.

"Ralph was easy. What a piece of shit. He was all pissed up. I caught him coming out of a bar at noon. He was staggering all over the place. To my good fortune, he slipped down an alley between a bar and a pizza joint to take a leak. I hid behind a dumpster. He never saw me coming. I was in an out like a Ninja, but I ripped him up pretty bad. It's Layla's old man that has me worried."

"What?" I asked.

Rolando ran water into his hand and cleaned his face with a couple of rapid swipes.

"I stomped his nuts right in front of his old lady."

"When did you do that? Where were you?"

I handed him a small towel. He wiped his face vigorously and ran the towel through his thinning hair. I certainly wasn't happy that he did what he did, but I wasn't unhappy either. Rolando had a true sense of justice in his heart. I could tell that while he was worried, he was also quite satisfied.

"After beating down Ralph, I figured what the fuck. We're leaving town, right? I headed over to Layla's and I waited. When he came home, I walked straight up his driveway. He turned to face me and you know it was almost like he expected it. He held his hands out as if to ask me why, and I just popped him. He hit the ground and I went straight for his instrument of pain. I jumped on his filthy dick. His old lady was standing right in the doorway. 'That's for Layla!' I yelled."

Rolando's knuckles were bleeding again. I didn't know exactly what to say. I felt more like hugging him than anything else, but if Layla's mother called the police we were all in for some serious trouble, and if Layla or Mary found out it was Rolando, it could ruin everything.

"It's our secret," I said.

"No shit," he answered. "And dude, I'm sorry. I know you like peace, but I had to do it."

"I know," I said.

I escaped to the small store. Thankfully next to the single doses of aspirin there were band-aids that would cover up Rolando's bleeding knuckles. As I purchased the package with the loose change in my pants pocket I watched a police car slow at the light. I held my breath when it passed right on by.

"Everything all right?" the little Chinese guy behind the counter asked.

"Great," I said.

Rolando and I rejoined the party after going through our story for Rolando's bruised hand. We decided that he would blame his injury on working on a car with his nephew. It wasn't great, but it was all we had.

When we returned to the table in my apartment it was evident that Layla and Adam had grown much closer. They were discussing our plan to meet Bruce at the Cleveland show.

"It's simple. We bribe a security guard," Adam said. "Guys that make ten bucks an hour are the easiest ones to buy. We give the idiot guarding the door a hundred and he steps aside. Once we get into the back room good-looking people like us can smooth our way through. Those two slugs will have a problem, though."

Adam was pointing straight at me. "This must be Rolando," he said. He offered a fist bump that Rolando pretended not to notice.

"How about a beer?" Rolando asked.

"Where's Mary?" I asked as Layla retrieved a beer for Rolando.

"She's upset," Adam said. "Someone beat the living shit out of her ex," Adam explained to Rolando. "I'd like to shake the guy's hand."

Rolando extended his hand and Adam shook it. Luckily for all of us, Adam was clueless.

"Why don't we get on the road?" Adam asked. "We have to swing back to the airport to pick up our traveling limo van. Wait until you guys see this thing!"

Rolando slugged down his beer in one gulp.

"One thing before we go," I said. "I need to write to Anna."

I slipped into my bedroom and the sanctity of my computer. Mary was lying on my bed with a washcloth on her forehead. Her eyes were closed, but I knew that she was more likely meditating than sleeping.

"Do you mind if I use the computer?" I whispered.

"No, go ahead," she answered.

I sat in the chair and punched up my email account. Mary's breathing was even. I'd known her long enough to know not to push the subject. I started my message to Anna. Her California life was starting to even out a little bit, and although there were still moments when the trouble between Dan and Rachael was evident, they were still playing family. Dan was still in my place as Anna's daddy.

"Hi my little baby girl. Today I was thinking about you and my heart started to ache a little bit, but I pushed away my lonely thoughts by thinking of tickling you. Remember how I used to tickle you until you begged me to stop?"

I paused to think about Layla and the fear and pain caused by her miserable stepfather. I considered the moment when Rolando's boot came straight down on that idiot's balls.

"Whenever you feel lonely I want you to think of me, Anna. Think about how much I love you and how I'd do anything to make sure that no one ever hurts you. My love is as big as a redwood tree."

Mary stirred in the bed. She cleared her throat, and in a voice just above a whisper she said just five words.

"Ralph deserved it, you know?"

"I know," I said.

"Anna, our quote of the day comes from your Aunt Mary's favorite philosopher, Buddha. He once said; *Peace comes from within. Do not seek it without.*'"

"I don't know why I loved him," Mary whispered behind me. "I don't believe in violence, but I understand it sometimes."

"Sometimes you get what's coming to you," I said.

I turned my attention back to Anna's note.

"Our word of the day is *precarious*. That means dangerously lacking in security or stability. I love you, Anna. I miss you more every day. Love your bonus Daddy."

I hit send on my message. Adam was calling out to me.

"Let's go, fuck-face."

"I'm ready," I yelled back.

As I was getting up and out of my chair, Mary was by my side. She had moved across the room like a whisper. She leaned in and kissed me on the forehead.

"I won't say another word about this," she said. "But when you have him alone, do me a favor."

"Anything," I said.

"Thank Rolando for me," she said.

A tear rolled down her cheek.

"Now let's go meet Bruce."

CHAPTER 10 – THERE IN THE HIGH TREES LOVE'S BLUEBIRD GLIDES

No matter what anyone tells you, life is all about love. Actually, it's the pursuit of love that drives us in all areas, from all points-of-view, and at all times. We grow up wanting to be loved. We come of age needing to be loved, and we check out, in the end, wondering if we've loved enough.

As our limo van pulled out of the parking lot of a car dealership near the Buffalo-Niagara Falls International airport I was thinking a lot about love. From my vantage point in the very last row of seats I could see all the assembled gathering of my most recent attempt at stuffing love down my own throat.

Adam was behind the wheel. He had really gone all out in making this happen, but it had been easy for him. He threw a huge dollar amount at the problem, and the love followed. The van was a black Ford, 12-seater with tinted windows, and dark red interior. The seats were arranged so that all could either sit comfortably or even lie down in the back rows. Adam was wearing a white tennis cap as he steered along I-90 heading west towards Cleveland. The GPS was telling him where and when to turn, but having been on this road before in pursuit of Bruce, we all knew that it was pretty much a straight shot for roughly three hundred miles. Adam was singing loud and proud to the words of *Sherry Darling* from *The River* record. He loved trying to guess the lines and he occasionally got a word right. Despite the fact that Adam was apt to confusion about the lyrics his enthusiasm was contagious.

"Pass me a beer," Adam said, with a laugh, knowing that Mary had banned all drinking until the van was parked.

Still, as I considered Adam, I couldn't help feel sorry for my multi-million-dollar friend. His father had always been a colossal asshole to him, and his mother never wanted to rock the boat because she loved diamonds. Adam's ship was adrift in that land of aggravation.

Directly behind Adam was Mary. She had held up our departure with a listing of the rules that would allow us a trip of true spiritual renewal. There would be massages, Bible readings and deep philosophical discussions on our way to meet the Boss. She was dressed for the occasion as well. Her red, green and white blouse was adorned with crosses and the words *He Died for Us* covering most of the area of the shirt. She had made the shirt herself about twenty years ago. She treated that shirt as if it were alive. The love in my heart came with a true ache for Mary. She lived her life believing that it would all work out, but because of Ralph, and her dependency on him, it hadn't. I actually wondered what she dreamed about anymore. As she massaged Adam's shoulder from her spot directly behind his seat, I also considered if she'd ever truly find what she was looking for.

"Yo! fuck face!" Adam called out, lowering the volume on Bruce's *Wreck on the Highway.*

"Yes, my brother," I called back.

"I forgot to tell you that this van is yours when this little trip was over. I bought it outright after I saw that piece of shit you were driving around in."

"What am I going to do with a limo van?" I asked.

"Sell it," Adam said. "Buy what you want."

Adam turned the volume back up as one of his other favorites, *Cadillac Ranch*, began.

"I can sell it for you," Rolando said. "I'll take you car shopping. We'll get something that doesn't make you look like a loser."

I smiled at Rolando, but he wasn't looking for an answer. He dropped back to his sleeping position, and I considered what he had done for Layla and Mary. I was proud of him. Despite his tough guy exterior, however, I knew that there was a real soft guy inside. Rolando's pain may have been greater than all of ours combined. I wasn't sure that he really had any hope at all, but I did know that he would go down fighting.

All at once, Layla jumped up and out of her seat and headed back to my own personal row.

"You wanna' make out?" she asked me.

"I do," Rolando said as his head popped up over the seat.

"I'm good," I said, "but I patted the seat and Layla sat down beside me. As expected she reached out and grabbed my hand.

"My mom called and I told her about the trip," Layla said. "I couldn't believe it, but she told me to have a good time and asked me if I needed any money."

Rolando showed his face over the seat once more.

"How's your dickhead stepfather?" he asked.

"Mom didn't mention him, and I didn't ask," Layla said. "He's probably out sticking his thing somewhere."

"I doubt that," Rolando said, but he disappeared behind the seat once more. I saw a smile on his face just before it went from view.

"I've never felt better about life than I do right now," Layla said. "That's why I wanna' make out. I have so much energy!"

"Still here!" Rolando called out.

Layla was rubbing my hand vigorously. God, she was so pretty. She was way too young, as well.

"Tell me about your Mom," she said.

Just those five simple words made my heart ache. I most certainly wasn't ready to talk about losing my mother.

"I thought you were happy," I said. "That's a sad story."

Layla considered it for a long moment. Mary had switched the Bruce album from *The River* to *Magic*. Bruce was singing about *Radio Nowhere* asking the audience if there was anyone alive out there.

"The more I get to know you, the happier I am," Layla said.

"I swear to God," Rolando called out. "If you don't start kissing that broad I'm gonna' throw you out the back of the fucking van."

But I didn't start kissing her. Instead, I told her what I remembered most about my mother.

"She was always smiling," I said. "And she was always asking me if I needed anything. Mom got sick right after I was born, and it broke her heart that she couldn't have any more kids, but she told me that I was perfect, and that she never needed another one. I know she was sad a lot because she knew that the cancer would eventually get her, but we had thirteen years together. I watched her go from healthy and beautiful to bald and weak, but I never met a stronger person."

"You never will," Layla said.

Her head was resting on my shoulder. The scent of her perfume was overwhelming, and I looked to the spot where our hands met. What in the hell was going on between us? There was no logical sense to our relationship, but it continued to grow. It was love that I was chasing, but deep down, I really feared the pain that was going to eventually blossom out of our closeness.

"And your Dad went to shit when she died?" Layla whispered.

"He was gone way before she left," I said. "He drank a lot. He slept a lot. He actually hated being alive. I was at work when he shot himself. I had quit school to try and help him through, but when that call came, I listened to the police officer on the other end of the line.

'There's been an accident,' he said.

'He finally did it,' I answered.

For the first time in his life, he had succeeded."

"If he succeeded then dad can't be the reason you're a complete and utter failure," Rolando said cheerfully.

Layla started to voice a protest, but my laughter stopped her.

The music went silent and Mary stood up. She was holding a microphone in her hand and as she spoke the feedback nearly sent Rolando to the roof of the van.

"Sorry about that," she said. "Do you guys like our speaker system? Adam had this put in so we could all take the mic from time-to-time. I will be our master of ceremonies, but sooner or later we are all going to speak!"

Mary did a curtsey and laughed. It was the first time I'd heard her laugh since Ralph took his beating so I smiled along with her.

"I want to thank the Lord for allowing us all to come together for the next few weeks as we travel, safely, across the northeast. Jesus, please take us into your heart, allow us to find the love that we all need to survive in a world that sometimes seems strange. We thank you Lord for one another, and we trust in you to bring us hope. Thank you!"

Mary returned the mic to the holder and Bruce's voice once more filled the van.

"This is gonna' take some getting used to," Rolando said. "Between the endless rumblings of marble mouth and Billy Graham on the microphone I'm gonna' have to get high before I put one through my temple like Joseph's old man."

Once more Layla jumped to my defense, but it didn't matter. There was a smile in Rolando's voice, and I knew he was thankful to be along as well.

Adam navigated the van to the Eden-Angola rest stop about thirty miles south of Buffalo. I wasn't exactly sure why we were stopping so soon, but the final thing that Layla said before we pulled into the area would be the jumping off point for our first argument of the trip.

"I don't believe in God," she said. "I think it's all a lot of bullshit."

"Amen to that," Rolando agreed.

"Everyone off the bus!" Adam called out. "We will be doing a lot of stretching on this trip!"

I wish that I'd been quicker to exit my seat. Perhaps I would have been able to stop Layla from spouting her theological theories to Mary. Yet it was bound to happen sooner or later.

***

Evidently the argument started in the bathroom, but it was in full force by the time we stood in line for coffee. Rolando and Adam were at the gas pumps with the van. Rolando was washing the back window while Adam pumped the gas. I was stuck with Layla and Mary, waiting in line at Tim Horton's for a few cups of coffee.

"I'm just saying," Layla said. "If God is so loving and kind and merciful then why the hell is there so much evil?"

"God granted us free will. We are all free to make decisions about how to live life. In the end, He will judge us on how we went about making the right choices."

"Bullshit alert!" Layla announced. "God doesn't care about me. If He did I wouldn't have grown up like that. If He was kind and merciful my stepdad would have been crushed to death in a horrific accident. Your God let that go on for years and years. He let me suffer! I prayed to Him every night to make it stop and He didn't."

"It stopped now," Mary said. "You're with us now, right? God answers your prayers. Sometimes they aren't answered in the timeframe we like or to our satisfaction but they do get answered."

Mary was trying all of her best reassuring faces, but I knew that she was frustrated. To Mary the question of God wasn't up for debate.

"That's idiotic," Layla said. "You're just suggesting that whatever happens is God's plan. Good, bad, or indifferent it really doesn't matter. God is in charge and He loves me, right?"

"Right," Mary said.

"There ain't no God," Layla said. "It's all bullshit, like Santa Claus."

Thankfully we were next up in line. I tried to shift everyone's mind to coffee even offering to buy a basket of donuts. It didn't work.

"You have to feel God's joy," Mary said. "To have joy one must share it with others. I will spend this trip trying to share the peace I feel inside, no matter what happens on the outside. Obstacles can't crush me they only strengthen my resolve to be closer to God."

"What the fuck!" Layla yelled out.

Heads were turning in our direction. The young kid dressed in the brown and red uniform was looking at me for an answer.

"Can we get five medium coffees with cream and sugar on the side," I said.

"When did you learn how to talk like a Chinese fortune cookie?" Layla asked.

I'm not sure that Layla was really angry, but I knew Mary well enough to know that the discussion would have a lasting effect.

"I've found peace within," Mary said. "Only those free of resentment can truly find peace."

I squeezed Layla's hand to try and get her to stop talking. That didn't work either.

"No wonder Ralph beat you," Layla said.

It was obviously the absolute worst thing to say. Instantly Layla's hand went to her mouth as she tried, too late, to block the words from escaping. Mary did escape though. She turned on her heels and ran through the rest area nearly knocking a mother and a small child to the floor in the process of her flight. I paid for the coffee and we hustled out. We were just in time to hear the second fight of the day.

Rolando and Adam were standing toe-to-toe at the door to the van.

"Take it fucking back," Rolando shouted.

"I'm not taking it back," Adam said. "I said what I meant and I meant what I said."

I pushed between the two. Layla rushed by me to join Mary in the van. I was hoping she could put the God-discussion to rest.

"What happened?" I asked.

"Richie-Rich put down the attendant," Rolando said. "He told the guy, 'no wonder you pump gas for a living given your limited brain power.'"

"I was joking," Adam said to me. His smile was infuriating.

"Do you know that Rolando is a gas station attendant?" I asked.

Adam laughed. "I had a sneaking suspicion," he said.

It took all of my strength to hold back Rolando's charge. I was absolutely convinced that he would 'fucking kill the spoiled bastard,' but I was able to push Adam clear.

"Apologize now," I said.

Adam held his hands out in a surrender position. In a clearly mocking voice he said, "I'm sorry, Rolando. I won't do it again."

Rolando answered by not answering. He reached into his coat pocket and pulled out a small joint. He lit it as he stared Adam down. I wanted to mention that smoking pot in the parking lot of a public rest stop wasn't the best of ideas, but Rolando took three quick hits, and snuffed it out. He jumped into the van and made a beeline for the back seat.

"He's a tad sensitive," Adam whispered.

Ten minutes later we were back in the driving lane of I-90. Everyone was sitting alone. The music remained off. We were still over two hundred miles away from the Quicken Loans Arena and we were a long way clear of establishing the love we all so desperately needed.

I was nearly asleep when my cell phone blinked a text message to me.

"Hi, this is Anna. I just wanted to say 'Hi', so 'Hi.'"

"Hi, my little baby girl," I typed back. "You must have been thinking about how big my love is. Well, it is bigger than a jet airplane and it moves faster too, from my heart to yours. Always remember that it is better to conquer yourself than to win a thousand battles, my little girl. I'm on my way to see Bruce. We are going to stay at a campsite tonight near Cleveland and tomorrow night we are going to see him in concert. I'll send you some photos. Our word of the day is *esoteric*. That word means something that is difficult to understand. There are days when life is just plain esoteric. I love you. Hi to you."

"Yo, fuck face," Adam called out. "Do you remember when we saw Bruce on the *Tunnel of Love* tour at Nassau Coliseum in Long Island?"

"Great show," I called back.

"They played for four-and-a-half hours," Adam said.

"Twenty-seven songs," I called back. "It was April second in 1988. It was the day before Easter."

"*Adam Raised a Cain* was the third song," Mary said. "I remember how happy we all were that night."

My cell phone buzzed once more.

"I love you too," Anna wrote back. "Me and Mommy are going to try and call you tomorrow."

"The *Tunnel of Love?*" Layla asked. "Can we hear that one?"

"Great suggestion," I called out.

I turned to gauge Rolando's reaction in the last row of seats.

"Oh great, now marble mouth is going to teach us about love," he said.

But there was no mistaking Rolando's wry smile.

Chapter 11 – Getting Wasted in the Heat

Adam pulled the van into the American Wilderness Campground about thirty-five miles away from the arena in Cleveland. It was going to cost us about a hundred bucks to park in a spot with a lake site view, but we were ready for the party to start. Mary and Layla headed to the office to pay the fare leaving Rolando, Adam and me in the parking lot, drinking our first beer of the day.

"How've you been?" I asked Adam. "We joke around a lot, but you doing all right?"

"I'm good," Adam said. He took a sip of beer and a pull off of Rolando's discreetly handed joint.

"I'm still just trying to stay clear of the ill winds that gust all around me. The old man runs his business, my mother runs his life, and I'm just waiting them both out."

"You'll get everything when they go?" Rolando asked.

"I'm the heir apparent," Adam said. "Dad is fond of saying that he wouldn't let me supervise the wallpapering of a bathroom, but he is resigned to the fact that he's gonna' have to leave it to me."

"And he's a multi-millionaire?"

"Closer to billionaire," Adam said. "He's also a world-class douche bag."

But I had known all of that. What I really wanted was to get a grip on Adam's life itself. Was he happy? Would he leave Layla alone? Was he with us on the quest to meet Bruce just for kicks, or did he need it too?

"There are days when I want to put a bullet in my head," Adam said, "but don't we all get there from time-to-time?"

Rolando laughed.

"On the line to grab a billion dollars and you want to kill yourself?"

"Money is paper and ink, dude," Adam said. "When the people who are supposed to care for you are more thrilled with the concept of paper and ink than love and trust then it becomes more than a minor nuisance."

"Boo-fucking-hoo, I'm too rich," Rolando cried out. "I can see what a burden that can be."

Adam finished his beer and rooted around in the cooler for another. He'd been through such things on a daily basis. He shot an annoyed glance at Rolando.

"All right, *fat Man*. You don't mind if I call you *fat man*, do you?" Adam asked.

"No, that's fine," Rolando said. "You're good with *dick weed*, right?"

They shook hands.

"*Dick weed* meet *fat man*," I said.

Adam handed Rolando a second beer. I had only taken a few sips of mine so I was out of the exchange.

"Suppose, for an instant, *fat man* that you have everything you need in life on the financial front. Now what?"

"I surround myself with 'yes' men and beautiful women," Rolando said.

"You're still lonely," Adam said.

"I eat at the best restaurants in the world, go to every sporting event, and bet on every race," Rolando tried. His eyes were drifting towards the sky which was gunpowder grey and threatening rain.

"You're still lonely," Adam said.

"Yeah, but, fuck, you know," Rolando said.

Layla and Mary were heading back towards us. Mary was looking down at the paperwork. Layla appeared to be singing. She was too far away to hear, but I knew that it would sound like what an angel might sound like.

"Right now, for the first time in a lot of days, I don't feel lonely," Adam said. "That's what Bruce does for me."

Adam went to grab me in a headlock. I struggled clear.

"It's back to marble mouth again," Rolando said. "The guy sings songs for crying out loud."

"But it's what he sings about that's important," Adam said.

Adam didn't bother to finish his thought. Instead, he succeeded in running me down and when he had me in the headlock he whispered in my ear.

"That's love in front of you, *fuck face. D*on't let it go."

Layla's voice could finally be heard above the movement of the wind. She was singing *Out in the Street.*

***

Rolando was in charge of keeping the fire stoked and he took great pride in his job. The night air was chilled, but we sat around the fire in a big circle with red and blue Buffalo Bills blankets covering our legs. Layla was beside me on one side of the fire and Mary sat between *dick weed* and *fat man* on the other side. The beer was flowing nicely.

"Twenty-four hours, Joseph!" Mary called out. "In one days time we will be in the same location as Mr. Springsteen and his closest friends."

I raised my beer bottle as the thought of those opening moments stirred emotional unrest courtesy of my heart.

"Remember 1985 at the CNE Stadium in Toronto?" Adam asked.

I started laughing. It was a show that Adam had talked me into attending at the last minute. We scalped tickets in the parking lot, paying triple the price to see Bruce from the very last row of the event.

"That place was a freaking mob scene," Adam said. "There were at least a hundred thousand people there. Remember how excited I got when I finally was able to see Max swing a drum stick in the middle of the fourth song?"

Johnny 99," I said. As soon as the words left my mouth I wanted to snatch them back. Mary's head bowed.

"Now you did it," Adam said. "You had to bring up Ralph."

Layla and Rolando were lost. Adam allowed them to stay that way. He sang the opening line to Thunder Road, getting every word right. I joined in, singing line two.

Before long the three of us were on our feet screaming out the words to *Thunder Road.* We lost Adam's vocals midway through the song as he forgot the lyrics, but Mary was in full voice.

"You sing like Patty," I said, referencing Bruce's wife. Mary smiled.

"I hate Patty because she gets Bruce," she said, "while I got stuck with freaking Johnny 99."

Following our performance the sounds of the night took control once more. It was Layla who broke the momentary silence.

"I wasn't even born in 1985," she said. "But you guys just made me feel as if I were there. Can you imagine being as powerful as Bruce is?"

The question sounded like something Mary might pose as a starting point for conversation.

"Long after he's gone the world will be alive with what he did. His songs will live on. Kids will hear the music from their mothers and fathers. Radio and television will keep playing him. He will live on. How many people really get to live on like that?"

"And the beautiful Layla hits on exactly what I was trying to tell *fat man* earlier," Adam said.

I glanced over at Rolando. He had one eye on the fire and the other eye on the cooler of hot dogs and hamburgers. He had promised to cook for us one more time before we went to bed. I seriously doubted that Rolando gave two shits about Springsteen's lasting presence on planet Earth.

"What was that line you sang in that song there about being alone?" Rolando asked.

Instantly the lyrics to Thunder Road flickered through my brain. I had sipped quite a few beers, but thankfully I was able to retrieve them.

I knew just the line that Rolando was speaking about. Bruce sings early on about not being turned away because he doesn't want to be alone again.

"Yeah, that's it," Rolando said. "That's some powerful shit, dude. Maybe if you break down marble mouth's words for me I will actually enjoy this."

Rolando grabbed a hold of two logs and carefully, from a kneeling position, placed them in the perfect spot at the base of the fire.

"You see when the people who bring you into this world are more wrapped up in their own silly lives it's tough to learn how to think about anyone but yourself."

Rolando said the words but they may have come straight from Adam's mouth. Two men who were results of sets of parents on opposite ends of the social ladder were now undeniably connected.

"Amen to that, brother," Adam called out.

Layla's hand felt warm in mine. She worked my hand as she held it making circles with her thumb, and holding it for all that it was worth.

"The energy of the mind is the essence of life," Mary said. "What we do together, just sitting here talking, is make sense of what is basically nonsensical, but in a gentle way, we can shake the world."

Her words hung in the air, and it seemed that each of us, gathered around that fire, snatched them and made them our own.

"I'm right too. Even if I speak like a fortune cookie," Mary said. "Somewhere along the way every single one of us has been bitten by a snake filled with venom."

"And going to see Bruce Springsteen allows us to spit that venom out," Rolando said. "Well then mother-fuckers, let's do this."

Rolando went to the cooler. He made his way around the

fire handing each of us a new beer. He pulled the hot dogs and hamburgers from their resting place and retrieved the small grill from the back of the van.

"Joseph, music please," he said. "Something a little rowdy from the new album, please. What's that hopes and dreams one?"

"*The Land of Hopes and Dreams*," I said.

"That's the one. People get ready, the train is coming," Rolando said.

We had our last member of the Springsteen tour group officially on board. Just before I hit play on the I-pod Mary took control of the toast.

"From here on out we are going to be known as Mary and Joseph's: We Are Alive Traveling Circus. As JFK once said, 'Do not pray for an easy life; pray to be stronger men and women.'"

Mary raised her beer high in the air. The fire crackled at that moment and I know that I wasn't the only one who jumped.

"Hey, Mary and Joseph and Adam," Layla called out. "I never even thought of that."

We all laughed a bit too loudly. We chugged our beers, and there was no mistaking the feeling in the cold air. We *were* alive. I almost forgot, for a split-second, that Rachael and Anna hadn't called.

***

I wish I could say that sleeping in the back of the van was fun. The seat just wasn't wide enough to lay side-by-side with Layla so we were practically on top of one another. I offered to move to another seat but she wanted me with her. We slept fitfully. Once more the last thing that Layla said to me before she slipped off to sleep was what I dwelled on all night as I tossed and turned.

"I want the good times to remain," she had whispered.

Layla's words stuck with me for the entire night as I listened to Rolando and Adam's snoring contest at the front of the bus. Those words ate into me, one by one, because I knew that there was no way to truly hold on. My life's experience had told me that for every three days of happiness there were ten days of hurt. That was the simple math. Yet today promised to be one of the great days. We would end our day with the concert, and there was no way that could turn into a bad experience.

By noon we were all up and around. Rolando had started the fire and the grill and without even asking he prepared a breakfast of eggs and pork sausage. Evidently he had found the convenient store and had taken it upon himself to get the day rolling. There was little doubt that Rolando was showing the most surprising of attributes. Who knew that he was such a kind and gentle soul? Of course, he was finished with his third beer by the time the eggs were ready.

We ate quickly, discussing our plan to bribe a security guard at the arena. Adam was looking over a print out of the arena floor that he'd stashed in his bag. Our tickets were prime seats in section 109 with a wide open view of the stage.

"If we come in through the doors on Huron Street we can work our way around. The bus for the band will probably enter off of Ontario Street going straight into the arena near the stage door. We need to get to the guy at that door. It might be costly, but every man has his price," Adam said.

Mary cleared her throat. I knew that she was about to piss all over

Adam's plan.

"How much do you figure?" she asked.

"At least five hundred," Adam said. "Maybe even a grand."

"Do you remember my rule?" Mary asked. "Whatever money we spend has to come out of the general fund. We only have $1,500 in that fund. You are not buying our way to see Bruce. That would be wrong."

Adam looked at me. I shrugged my shoulders and smiled.

"That's kind of stupid," Adam said. "I have access to money. I'm part of the group. Why don't we just use our advantages?"

"You know perfectly well why," Mary said. "This meeting will be one of chance that is controlled by the universe. We can put ourselves into position but we will not manipulate the scene through greed and deceit."

From Layla's reaction I knew that she was on Mary's side. Her beautiful face was alive with expression as she nodded in agreement.

"The world is built on greed and deceit," Adam said. "You think Bruce would sing his songs for free?"

"Actually I think he might," Mary said, and she moved away from the fire signaling an end to the conversation. "If we are going to bribe the security guard it will be a corporate effort. We have to ask ourselves if that is how we want to spend our money because Adam will not be bailing us out through the course of this trip."

"The mighty Oz has spoken," Rolando called out.

"Well then," Adam began, "Let's get to the arena and see if anything else shakes out."

There was just one more piece of business to take care of on the way to my perfect day. I answered my ringing cell phone to silence my *Badlands* ringtone.

"Joseph, it's Rachael," she said into my ear.

CHAPTER 12 – YOU CAN'T SHUT OFF THE RISK AND THE PAIN

"It's not working out," Rachael said. She gasped for a breath of air that didn't seem to be there.

I was holding Layla's hand with my right hand. The cell phone pressed to my left ear felt as if it weighed a hundred pounds.

"Are you there?" Rachael asked.

"I'm here," I said. "I'm always here. Tell me about it."

There was no mistaking that Rachael was crying. She cried through the telling of the story, making mention that Dan was out on the town most every night.

"He's screwing around, and the worst part of all of it is that he doesn't care if I know. I asked him about it the other night and he laughed. He wondered if I was going to run back into the arms of 'the biggest loser on the planet.'"

Adam and Mary were dancing in front of me, trying to coax me into the van so that we could get to the show. Layla was leaning in tight, begging me with her body movements to just get off the phone. Rolando emitted a loud fart that told me of his displeasure about being held up. If it were ever the time to argue the point about being the world's biggest loser I had some evidence in my favor that there were others in competition with me.

"How does he treat Anna?" I asked.

Rachael hesitated, and in that hesitation I knew the answer. I felt my blood go cold.

"He's her father," Rachael said. "But there's not a lot in the way of affection. It hasn't gone as I planned."

I tried to turn away as Adam made a quick approach, but he was too quick. Adam grabbed the phone out of my hand as if I weren't even holding it.

"So sorry," he said, "but Joseph is on his way to see the Boss. He's gonna' have to call you back."

Adam handed the phone back to me. "Wrap it up!" he yelled.

Rachael's tone had definitely changed.

"You're back to chasing a rock star around the world?" She asked.

"We're going to a concert," I said.

"And when's the next one? Tomorrow? The day after?"

I didn't want to get defensive, but what else could I do?

"Should I have just sat in the apartment waiting for your call?" I asked.

"One question," Rachael said. "If I told you to pick us up at the airport in two hours, would you?"

It was a completely unfair question and one that was impossible to answer when I considered Layla's warm hand inside my own. It was my turn to hesitate.

"Fuck you," Rachael said, and the line went dead in my ear.

I said her name three times and then I looked at the phone as if it were a live thing. "She hung up," I said.

"Good," Layla said.

But it just wasn't that simple. In my mind's eye I saw Anna sitting in that beautiful home an entire country away. In my vision, my beautiful little girl was crying.

"The dogs on Main Street howl!" Rolando called out.

"Because they understand," I whispered back.

Yet there wasn't a single thing that I was capable of understanding.

***

We returned to the road with just a half an hour of travel between us and the arena and hopefully our date with destiny. Adam got me thinking about Bruce again by cranking up the *Wrecking Ball* record and we sang loud and proud through *Easy Money*. We dreamed about getting there early enough to see Bruce walking around the perimeter of the arena. There were reports that he'd done such a thing years ago on the *Born in the USA* tour.

"Remember when we ate at that stand at the CNE in Toronto because they had a sign that said Bruce ate here?' Adam asked. "*Fuck -face* asked the lady what Bruce ate and she said a Rueben so he ordered one."

"Maybe he did," I said.

"Yeah, he stepped out of his dressing room and ordered a grease-filled Rueben from a toothless carny. Damn, you've always been a goofy-fuck!"

I was thinking about the fact that I had actually believed the woman. Perhaps that was what was wrong with me. I'd always believed in everything, and expected the best of people. When Dan returned to Rachael and Anna's life I just went along for the ride, actually believing that he would treat her right and that their family would be whole.

"Joseph is kind of naïve," Rolando said. "In fact, some might say clueless."

I didn't get much of a chance to answer because a loud shriek from Mary caused all of us to jump in our seats.

"Stop the van! Stop right now!" she screamed.

Adam didn't hesitate. He pulled the van over on I-90 and we drifted to the side of the road in a cacophony of blaring horns.

"What's wrong?" Adam yelled. He turned Bruce down and unbuckled his seatbelt to get to Mary who was struggling out of hers.

"A roadside memorial," Mary cried out, and before any of us could react she was out of the car and running down the shoulder of the road.

"That broad is bat shit crazy," Rolando said.

Yet we all followed Mary to the spot just off the shoulder of the road where wreaths of red and white flowers and wet and dirty stuffed teddy bears sat below a crucifix with a name on it: Natalie Myers, 17.

"We need to pray," Mary said. "We have to be a small part of sending her spirit off to a better world."

"Are you fucking kidding me?" Adam asked.

Mary removed a small plaque of dedication that was stuffed between a grimy white bear and a cache of flowers. She read the words to us.

"Natalie was a beautiful girl, inside and out. Her life ended on this stretch of road as her car was struck head-on by a drunk driver who was heading the wrong way on I-90. Natalie's dreams were snuffed out by a horrible crime. We will not let her spirit die. This memorial is a testament to the love we feel for our beautiful friend, daughter, sister and niece. As you read these words, please pray for Natalie's soul, and know that while her body has left, her love never will. We love you, Natalie."

Mary was in tears as she finished the reading. She held her hands out and without even thinking we formed a circle of prayer in front of the memorial.

"We love you, Natalie. We share in your loss, and tonight we will carry your spirit with us, as we laugh, dance and sing. We will dedicate our fun tonight to your lovely spirit and we look forward to the day when we will meet you in heaven."

"Bait shit crazy," Rolando whispered.

Our heads were bowed. Traffic was flying by. The van, with its hazard lights flashing, was parked askew on the shoulder of the road.

"Back to the van," Adam said, "before it gets demolished."

"I'm so sad for that girl," Layla said. "She never got the chance to live a happy life."

Once more, my mind went to Anna and the fact that she was sad.

"I hope when I'm gone someone misses me," Layla said as a sob threatened to take control. "I hope that I find someone to love me."

"I love you already," I said. It was an automatic response, but when I said it I also knew that I meant it.

"I love you too," Layla answered and then she broke down.

We loaded back into the vain. Mary chose *We Are Alive* from the new record, and as she played it, I thought of all that we leave behind when we go. Mary might have been bat shit crazy but she was right about one thing; when love is given, it can never be taken away. It makes its way around the universe in a never-ending circle, for all time. As we covered the last few miles to the arena, I felt the undying love of Natalie Myers' life.

***

Believe it or not, six hours before the show, there was traffic all around the arena. We parked in the closest parking lot, paying thirty dollars for the privilege to do so. Mary paid for parking out of the general fund.

"We have a little over twelve-hundred left," she said. "Let's be smart on how much we bribe the guy."

We were at the back of the open van, eating lunch meat sandwiches and sipping beer. Layla, of course, was at my right side, tapping her feet in time to *Death to My Hometown*, a rocking song from the new record.

"I have an idea," she said. "As long as Joseph doesn't mind, why don't I play with the guard's little weenie? I can get us by him in about three minutes, guaranteed."

"I love the idea!" Rolando said. "We'll all blow him. It won't cost us a dime!"

"You'd really do that?" I asked.

"What's the difference?" Layla asked. "I've been used and abused for years. I get him off; we get to meet Bruce, it's all good."

Adam and Mary were on a scouting trip around the arena. When they returned they were as fired up as I've ever seen them.

"It's a done deal," Adam said. "We met a big black security guard standing on Huron Street. This dude is humungous."

Mary was nodding along.

"Anyway, he said that for two hundred bucks and our five tickets he'd get us a meet and greet with the band and seats in the lower bowl. He said for an extra hundy he'd make sure we got into the pit close to the stage."

Thankfully Rolando was skeptical enough for the both of us.

"Sounds like a load of shit to me," he said.

But it was Mary who was swaying me. She shook off Rolando's skepticism with her unwavering spirit.

"His name is Alex. He has three children, and he's actually a part of Bruce's road show. He's worked with him since the *Darkness* tour. We did our homework."

"Tell me you still have our tickets," Rolando said.

"We gave them up," Adam said proudly. "Beer me, please. We have to meet Alex at the side door at six o'clock. We'll shake Bruce's hand, kiss Patty on the cheek, and watch the show from his feet. You'll see."

"Never happen," Rolando said.

"Shut-up," Layla said. "Why do you pee all over everything?"

At ten minutes after six, we stood in front of the door where we were supposed to meet Alex. To Mary and Adam's ultimate surprise, their new friend wasn't there.

"What the fuck?" Adam asked. He was swinging a half-filled can of Budweiser. I wanted to mention that walking around with a can of beer was frowned upon in most cities, but I stayed quiet. I was either within minutes of meeting my idol or we were about to be completely shut out.

"I can't believe you gave our tickets away to a fake security guard," Rolando said.

"He wasn't fake," Mary cried. "He had a walkie-talkie and a badge."

"I had a walkie-talkie and a badge when I was seven," Rolando said. "How did I get mixed-up with a goofy fucking gypsy and stupid fucking rich guy?"

Layla and I made our way to a bench a few hundred feet away from the simmering scene. Adam was wearing an old Bruce shirt from the *Human Touch* tour. Mary was in full Little Steven dress, including a red and white bandana. We couldn't hear their words but they were gesturing loudly at the side door.

"Rachael wants back in, doesn't she?" Layla asked.

"I'm not sure," I said.

"What would she make of me?" Layla asked.

"Not sure again," I said. "I don't even know what to make of you."

Layla's pretty face was upturned to look into my eyes.

"I know what you mean," she said. "We have to figure this all out on this trip. Eventually we'll need to get on with our lives."

All at once I saw the behemoth of a man that had to be Alex. He opened the side door to Mary, Adam and Rolando. They started shouting to us.

"We're on our way to meet Bruce," I said. "Something tells me we're going to figure it all out." I kissed Layla flush on the lips and we ran for the door.

"Quiet! Quiet!" Alex instructed us. "I can get fired for this."

We followed him down the long dark arena hallway. There were a few vendors setting up for the show but otherwise the lights were down as it was still an hour away from doors open. We headed to a door that was marked 'No Re-Admittance.'

"I can't promise that Bruce will be by before the show," Alex said, "but someone from the band will definitely pop their head in. If you don't shake the Boss' hand before the show, come and find me afterwards and I'll make sure you get an audience."

"What did you do with our tickets?" Rolando asked.

Big Alex just groaned. His groan sounded more like a growl than anything else. He turned to Mary and Adam.

"We can call the whole thing off if your grease ball friend has a problem," he said.

"He doesn't have a problem," Adam said.

After staring down Rolando for a full minute Alex opened the door and we were led into a dark room that looked more like a closet than anything else. There was barely enough room for all of us to stand side-by-side. There were a couple of mops and some cleaning supplies stuffed into the corner. There was a huge grey door on the backside of the room.

"The way it works is that you hold tight," Alex said. "Sometimes the band doesn't walk this hallway until it is just about show time, but they are aware that their biggest fans are stowed away for a quick shake of the hand and they are real accommodating."

"Do you know Bruce?" Layla asked.

"I've known him for years," Alex said. "He's the best."

I couldn't tell you how excited I was. I hugged Mary and Adam for all that I was worth, and I might have cried if it hadn't been for Rolando and his dark eyes of doubt.

"This is happening," I cried.

We waited in the closet until we could hear the other fans filing into the arena. We hung out there until the music was queued and blasted through the speakers. Bruce's shows always featured great warm-up music because there was never an opening act. We worked our way through *Thunder Road*, singing it out at the top of our lungs. Rolando only sang the line about not wanting to be left alone. We simply waited for Bruce, or Patty, or Nils, or Little Steven to open that door and wish us well. It was all we were searching for. As I kissed Layla on the mouth, I thought of Anna and Rachael and all of the pain. I thought of losing my mother and father, and how I'd never truly made it through that. It was all about to change. I was waiting for a moment…

…that never came.

At seven-thirty Rolando's anxiousness was becoming palpable.

"How long are you dumb fucks going to stand in a closet?" he asked.

"You're standing here too," I said.

"You know what Alex is doing right now?" Rolando asked. He was pacing the three feet of floor allotted to him. "He's sitting in our seats with four of his fucking friends drinking a beer that he bought with the two hundred dollars spending money you gave him."

"You're wrong!" Mary screamed.

But it turns out that Rolando wasn't wrong. At precisely eight-fifteen we heard the crowd groan as the house lights went down. Adam started to beat on the door that we had been led through. Rolando pushed open the door at the back of the room. It led to the street.

"Mother-fucker!" Adam screamed.

We had sat in a closet for two hours. We had trusted life and been burned by it. Again.

***

A half an hour later I was between Layla and Mary in the very top row of the arena. Bruce was but a speck on the stage some two hundred feet below. We had paid a scalper a hundred bucks apiece for the seats. Rolando and Adam skipped the show in an effort to find Alex. Rolando was cursing our stupidity all the way. Bruce was great, of course, but as he sang the words about it being nice if dreams came true I had a whole new appreciation.

Chapter 13 – A Thin White Line

I typed my message to Anna into my phone and hit send before even thinking about it. As I read it over I was sort of ashamed of myself for allowing my disappointment with life to spill over into her troubled days.

"To my little baby girl. Our word of the day is *caprice*. It means a sudden or unpredictable change. Unfortunately, beautiful, that is usually what is normal about life. Whenever you think you have it all figured out something will come along to mess it all up and crush your dreams. When that happens to you I want you to remember that I really love you. I'm with Aunt Mary as we travel around on a little road trip. She always tells me about Buddha, and so our quote for today comes from him. He once said, *Do not dwell in the past; do not dream of the future; concentrate the mind on the present moment.* I love you, Anna. Always and forever."

Unfortunately for all of us the present moment was a darkened, silent van on a crowded highway as we tried to escape Cleveland and the disappointment of a mostly lost night. The excited chatter of the show between Mary and Layla stopped the moment we arrived at the van. Rolando and Adam were seated on the hood drinking warm beer on the cold spring night. At least they weren't fighting. Somewhere along the line Rolando had forgiven Adam his stupidity. Yet now, we were traveling back to Buffalo in a sort of stunned silence.

Layla was on my left shoulder, of course. She was wearing a pink *Wrecking Ball* tee-shirt, and if it were all possible she looked even more beautiful to me now. The sound of her softly snoring beside me sent my heart into a bit of a tizzy, but my earlier conversation with Rachael had kick-started a head-on collision crashing in my guts. I considered my next text message, but just as I'd done with the message to Anna, I wrote it and sent it quickly.

"Of course I'd take you back," I wrote.

We were twenty minutes out of Cleveland when Mary stood up and grabbed the microphone. She was holding a small grey box in her hands.

"Good evening fellow travelers," she said. Her voice was a little raspy from having screamed from the rafters to try and get Bruce's attention.

"Some may believe that tonight was a setback on our journey, but I have been thinking that the path to spiritual awareness is filled with unknown obstacles. We tripped on a couple of huge rocks tonight because of mistakes that were made."

"By a gypsy and a spoiled rich kid," Rolando called out.

"We will not pass judgment," Mary said.

"I will," Rolando answered.

"Yet the ladder of success is best climbed on the rungs of opportunity and of course, success is how high you bounce once you hit bottom."

Mary made a grand gesture of opening the grey box. She counted the money in the backdrop of the overhead light.

"Minus the money we paid Alex and the cost of scalping the tickets for our extreme balcony seats, plus the thirty-pack of beer for Rolando we now have five-hundred and thirty-seven dollars left."

"I'll get the money back in the box," Adam said.

"No!" Mary yelled back. "Whatever happens happens. We're gonna' ride the adventure to the end. If we need more money we have to earn it."

"Bat-fucking-shit crazy," Rolando muttered.

"Like Bruce told some of us tonight, hard times come and hard times go. The man swimming against the stream knows the strength of it. Ambition is putting a ladder to the sky. We are still climbing."

Mary croaked out the chorus to *Born to Run* and although I didn't feel much like doing it I moved a groggy Layla off my shoulder and moved to the front of the bus where I shared the mic with her. Mary didn't sit down again until we told her that we were still with her on the mission to make it all work. Rolando answered with another audible passing of gas, but then he pumped his fist high in a sarcastic salute. We all settled in and drifted towards sleep as Adam moved the van along the dark highway.

***

The sound of the van lurching to the side of the road was what stirred me from my sleep. What I had missed was the long debate about whether or not to pick up the hitchhikers. Adam had been against it. Mary, of course, wanted to help get the black man and his gypsy-looking, pale white woman out of the rain. Mary won the argument.

"Whatsoever you do to the least of my brothers," Mary said as the side door opened and the black man led his girl into the seat beside Rolando.

"What the fuck? Are we running a bus service?" Rolando asked.

"'Sup, brother?" the black man asked. He held his fist out for a pump that Rolando wasn't in any mood to return.

"Sup?" Rolando asked. "Is that short for supper? Sit down and talk to someone other than me please."

The black man turned his attention to me.

"The name is William," he said. "My friends call me Billy. I'd be honored if you called me Billy."

He extended his fist to me and I tapped knuckles with him.

"This lovely creature is my soul mate, the incomparable Miss Missy."

"Hi Missy," I said. I repeated the knuckle tapping gesture with her.

Miss Missy was shaking the rain off her light black coat. When she smiled I made a mental note not to stare at her three missing teeth. I wondered if drug abuse were the cause of such decay. Billy tossed a duffel bag on the seat in front of us. He knocked the money box to the floor of the bus and he leaned across to pick it up and place it beside his bag.

"Where are you coming from on this dark and dreary night?" Missy asked.

"Springsteen concert," I said.

Mary had joined us and was leaning over the seat taking in everything about her new pet projects. Layla was still snoring softly on my left arm.

"Who dat?" Billy said.

"Bruce Springsteen," Mary said. "The rock star."

"Oh! The old dude," Missy said.

"He's still alive?" Billy asked.

It was going to be a long night. Billy's next sentence promised an even longer sentence.

"I'm a rap star," he said. "Rap is where it's at."

"You can't spell crap without r-a-p," Rolando called out from his seat.

"That's awfully white of you," Missy said.

Suddenly I became aware of the fact that pulling to the side of the road to offer a ride might not have been such a grand idea. I glanced out the side window to the mile markers racing by. We were approaching Erie, Pennsylvania and I saw signs for Gannon University.

"What the fuck does that mean?" Rolando asked.

"Just saying it's a bit intolerant," Missy said. "Rap is an art form. Are you telling me that Eminem isn't more talented than the fossil you guys went to see tonight?"

Rolando was sitting straight up now. He cleared his throat, raised one cheek, and farted as loudly as he could muster.

"Eminem is lily white," he said. "And he sucks. In fact, there might be something seriously wrong with him."

"Oh, it's on now, bitch!" Billy said with a laugh in his voice. "You know what I'm, saying?"

"Bitch?" Rolando said. "Did you just call me a bitch?"

"Simmer down," Adam called from the front of the van. He turned up the volume on *Lucky Day* from the *Working on a Dream* record.

"Is that Bruce Springstein?" Billy asked. "The big white Jew?"

"He isn't Jewish," I said. "It's Springsteen. He's of Irish, Dutch and Italian descent."

"A cracker," Missy said.

"*You're* a fucking cracker!" Rolando screamed.

"It doesn't matter anyway," Mary said. "We are all people. We don't see black and white or Jewish or Italian. What does it matter?"

Billy started laughing uproariously. When he moved in the seat I saw a small bag of white powder in his coat pocket. I decided to try and get the conversation back to a comfortable spot.

"So have you had any of your songs recorded?" I asked.

"We've done three albums," Billy said. "All freestyle shit, you know what I'm saying?"

"Why do you do that?" Rolando asked.

Billy turned to face Rolando. The slow movement of Billy's head told me that he mostly likely had tried some of the contents of the bag.

"Do what?" he asked.

"Say, 'You know what I'm saying?'" Rolando asked. "You make a statement and then you attach that question to it. It's fucking stupid. You know what I'm saying?"

Billy laughed again. When he shifted in his seat a second time I saw a knife. When I looked up after making the discovery I could see that Mary had also noticed the problem.

"Can you do a song for us?" Mary asked nervously. "We have a microphone."

"No," Rolando said. "I don't wanna hear his senseless shit."

146

But perhaps Mary had been onto something. If we could get Billy to sing perhaps he'd refrain from slicing us all to pieces.

"Do it! Do it! Do it!" Miss Missy cried out. "Oh, he's so talented!"

Billy made a grand gesture of getting himself ready for his appearance.

"Three albums, huh?" Rolando said. "It's a little surprising but I've never heard of you. Springsteen's third album was *Born to Run. Do* you know what I'm saying?"

"What's your name?" Billy asked Rolando.

"None of your business," Rolando said. "I don't want you to work it into your performance."

This really wasn't going very well. Layla stirred beside me and when she opened her eyes and spotted the skinny black man standing just a few feet away she let out a blood-curdling scream, which caused Miss Missy to scream, which made Mary gasp. I comforted Layla as Billy grabbed hold of the microphone. Adam turned Bruce down, and the performance started.

There were a lot of gestures and some gurgling, scratching, sounds coming from Billy's throat. He was dancing in the center aisle and all of our eyes were on him.

"Holy fuck!" Rolando cried out. "He's having a seizure."

"From the new disc," Billy said.

My name is Billy and I'm just so bad. I be the baddest man you ever had. My tool is long and fat and wide and I did my bitch until she cried. I love me some women, hot and fine, like Stevie Wonder says, 'I fuck 'em till they blind.' I'm the greatest man of all-time Jesus comes to me looking for wine.

"Stop it! Just stop it!" Mary cried out.

I was sure that it was the line about Jesus that had tipped Mary over the edge. Adam jerked the wheel and stomped the brakes as the van filled with shrieks of anguish from the women, and then boisterous laughter from Rolando.

"There's something fucking wrong with you," Rolando guffawed. "I've never heard anything dumber than that."

Rolando was absolutely right, of course, but his laughing jag was driving Billy and Miss Missy crazy. Adam sensing that there was trouble coming was out of his seat and headed to Billy. In one motion he grabbed hold of Billy and lifted him off his feet before Billy could get his hands on his knife.

"Leave him alone!" Miss Missy cried as she beat Adam's back.

"Do something," Layla said to me, but I was frozen to my spot in the seat.

Mary opened the side door. Billy hit the street with a thud and Miss Missy soon followed with the duffel bag in tow. The string of obscenities that flowed from both of their mouths would have made Satan blush. I'm sure that Rolando would have followed them out the door in a fit of rage had he not been laughing so hard.

"I'm gonna' piss myself," he called out. "'Jesus comes to me looking for wine', that's fucking priceless."

***

The next half an hour was filled with chatter about our rap friends. Mary provided a lecture, through the microphone, about not judging others and the cultural differences between us and Billy.

"Those who are free of resentful thoughts will surely find peace," Mary said.

Her diatribe was interrupted by the cheer that went up when we crossed into New York State, and a ringing cell phone that when pressed to her ear made Mary go pale.

"Ralph is back in the hospital. He called the cops on Rolando," she said. "The dumb bastard just tipped me off that they will be waiting for us at Joseph's apartment."

"Great, where do we sleep tonight?" Adam asked. "I need a damn bed."

"We can get a hotel room," Layla offered.

Mary bent down below the seat to grab the money box. As she rifled through it her expression changed. "Son-of-a-pup."

"They stole our fucking money, right?" Rolando asked.

I got to my feet and looked into the open box. The tickets were still there, but there wasn't a single dollar in the box.

"Looks like we'll be earning our own way a lot sooner than we thought," Mary said.

"Bat shit crazy," Rolando called out.

We hit the exit to my apartment. Adam slowed considerably as we cruised on by. There was a police car parked in the driveway.

"The dogs on Main Street howl!" Rolando called out.

"Shut-up," I answered.

CHAPTER 14 –TRUDGING THROUGH THE DARK

We spent the night at the Economy-Lodge Motel on Milestrip Road in Blasdell. We pooled the money we had left in our pockets covering the room with sixty dollars left over. Following the Buffalo show we had three more cities to cover and triple shows in New Jersey. Sixty dollars wasn't going to cut it.

In the late morning we shrugged off the grime of the road at the continental breakfast in the lobby. My neck was stiff and swollen from my night on the floor beside Layla. She slept between me and Rolando with Adam and Mary getting the beds.

"I still don't get it," Rolando said. "The two people who fucked up the Cleveland experience got the beds and I had to sleep on the floor like an Irish setter. I'm pretty sure I know who better make amends tonight. I better at least get to see old marble mouth sing."

Layla dumped about eleven packets of sugar into her small cup of coffee. Even tired she looked wonderful to me, but there was something different about her this morning. She was definitely down about something and I couldn't put my finger on it.

"So, here's the plan," Mary said. "It was Adam's idea, but it's brilliant."

Adam was at the front desk, flirting with the middle-aged woman as he checked us out of the room. I knew that it was just a matter of time before Adam tried to pick up a woman somewhere along the way and part of me hoped that he'd succeed so that he wouldn't eventually set his sights on Layla.

"I'm going to set up a fortune teller's booth a few streets away from the arena." Mary made the announcement as if we would all jump up and hug her, but she was greeted only with silence.

"Think of it, Joseph, like Madame Marie in the song *Sandy*.

"You're fucking Madame Marie?" Rolando asked.

"Yes, but we are going to need all of us. Layla and Adam will get customers to the table. Joseph collects the money and I'll use my Tarot cards to predict the future. We're thinking ten bucks a reading."

"You are *out* your fucking mind," Rolando said slowly emphasizing each word. "What are we going to do with the ten bucks you raise?"

Yet Mary was unflappable in her belief. She was measured and collected and before long her enthusiasm drew Layla into her plan. Rolando battled back, voicing his displeasure through guttural sounds that escaped a couple of different orifices, but he finally conceded.

"You're so calm," he said to Mary, "that you would probably do needlepoint with your hair on fire."

"I'm focused," Mary said.

I reached beside me to take Layla's hand, but she shrugged me off. "I need more sugar," she said.

Twenty minutes later, after dropping Rolando, Layla and Mary near the arena in downtown Buffalo; I sat in the passenger seat as Adam drove towards my apartment. We were going through the list of items we needed for the fortune teller show and as I compiled the list Adam opened up for the first time in years.

"I got a girl pregnant," he said. "I was in Omaha, Nebraska of all places trying to do my job. I'd checked into a downtown hotel and immediately went to the bar. The girl behind the bar, Theresa, served me drinks all afternoon and banged the shit out of me all through the night. Three months later, she called with the news. Two months after that she was gone, the child was gone, and so was about a hundred grand of my old man's money. Dear old Dad settled everything with a couple of scratches of the pen."

I didn't know exactly what to say to any of it. Given the way that Adam had lived his life it wasn't all that much of a shock, but his reaction to it certainly was.

"I wanted that kid," Adam said. "When Theresa told me she was pregnant I was actually thrilled, but Dad didn't want to hear of my intentions. He lectured me about personal responsibility, grilled me about bad publicity, and in the end, paid her to abort the child and go the fuck away. Theresa took the deal."

"You're going soft on me," I said. "The old Adam wouldn't have given any of this a second thought. Are you thinking of finding someone special?"

Adam laughed. We were listening to *The River* album and he paused long enough to add some volume to one of his favorite songs, *Ramrod*. He turned the volume down after the second verse. He pulled the van into the parking lot of the Rite-Aid drug store that was about three blocks from my apartment.

"We'll walk down to your place and get the lay of the land," he said. "If the cops are staking out the place looking for Rolando we'll have to decide if grabbing the card table and Mary's gypsy shit is worth it."

"Why don't we just go to the ATM?" I asked. "Mary might be just a bit around the bend on this one."

"That's what I'm saying," Adam said. "I don't want money to be the easy way out anymore. I'm all with Mary on this now. It's time I figured out things on my own."

"Wow, you are going soft on me," I said.

"Don't get me wrong," Adam said. "I'd still fuck a tree if I knew there was a hot broad standing behind it, but little by little, I'm growing up."

We walked slowly down the street, looking around each corner for the sign of a police car. Before long we were at the convenience store where Rolando worked in his life before Bruce.

"Looks like we're all clear," Adam said. "Let's get right in and right out."

Mary had provided very specific directions on where she'd left her gypsy shit. Adam found the decks of Tarot cards in the living room area and I stuffed a bag with the red and green scarves and purple and flower gowns that would provide Mary with the specific look needed. The only thing we couldn't put our hands on immediately were the fake gold bracelets and the large hoop earrings. Perhaps if we'd been three minutes quicker we would have avoided the knock at the door.

"I'll handle it," I told Adam.

I peeled back the side curtain and looked directly into the eyes of an overweight, middle-aged, black woman cop. She was on her game because she was staring right back at me as if she'd expected that curtain to move.

"Fucking Rolando," Adam said. "You can't just go around beating the shit out of people."

I opened the door slowly and the black woman, who looked a little like Esther Rolle from the old television show *Good Times* offered a frown.

"Do you know where we can find Rolando Arroyo?" she asked.

"Last I heard from Rolando he was talking about hitting the road to New Jersey," I said. "I don't even know how to get a hold of him," I said. "What's this about?"

"We just need to talk with him," the woman said. Her voice was deep, and her intense gaze conveyed the idea that I best not fuck with her.

"I don't even know Rolando very well," I said. "He worked next door and I'd see him when I grabbed a paper, but nothing more than that."

I was all in on it now, but what else could I do. I wanted her to explain what she knew about the beatings, but Esther Rolle wasn't talking much. She was content to just stare me down.

"You let Rolando know that the man he beat in the back alley of a bar is in intensive care. We *will* find him."

I was never very good at poker. I thought of Ralph and all the damage that he'd caused Mary and doing so sent my Adam's apple up and down in rapid fashion. Esther Rolle didn't miss the sign.

"And if you know more than what you're telling me, you're going to be sitting right beside him in the police car when he goes to jail."

I spread my hands wide and tried a smile that had no chance of being returned.

The cop turned her back, and I watched her huge ass cheeks shake as she approached the door to her cruiser.

"Have a great day," she said.

Back in the apartment Adam greeted me with the clanging bracelets and the hoop earrings. He had listened in on my exchange with the officer.

"Fuck!" he cried out. "What the hell do we do now?"

"None of us win unless we all win,'" I said.

"You won't do very well in jail," Adam said. "Your cellmate Bubba will devour you."

"Tell me about it," I said. "Maybe Mary is going to have to read my future first. Perhaps there's a card in the deck that tells me who my new husband is going to be."

We laughed, but it wasn't even a little funny.

Back downtown we immediately arrived to find the one thing that we really didn't want to see. Rolando was sitting on a bench in front of the First Niagara Center chugging a bottle of Miller Lite. He may as well have been carrying a sign that said, 'Arrest Me Now.'

"I'll take care of him," Adam said. "I grabbed a razor. I'll cut his hair and shave his face. Gonna' be hard not to make him look like Rolando, but I'll try. Go see what Madame Marie is up to."

I grabbed the bag of gypsy crap and headed towards Perry Street where Mary intended to set up camp. I was positioning the card table under my arm when it occurred to me that Adam was still within earshot. I thought of how he felt giving up that baby and how hard it must have been for him to tell me such a thing. I decided to hit him with a Mary-ism, courtesy of Buddha.

"Adam, *You, yourself, as much as anybody in the entire universe deserve your love and affection.*'"

Adam responded as I knew he would. He gave me the finger.

***

It was actually a beautiful day. The sun was riding high in a nearly perfectly blue sky. Bruce and the band were going to be on stage in a matter of hours, and for all I knew they were walking around town right now. My mind wandered, of course, and I pictured them walking up to Mary's table to have their fortunes read.

Mary and Layla had been working hard. The poster board sign was decorated with the fortune-tellers choices. Madame Marie was an expert in the oracle, love tarot, extrasensory perception, and of course, reading biorhythms. All of these readings were offered at ten bucks a pop and we barely got the table set up before our first customer stepped up in line. A middle-aged woman who looked as if she'd been one of the pretty girls in high school was looking for information.

"I've just been through a traumatic event," she said, "and I'd like some answers."

She set ten dollars on the table. Mary slipped into her gypsy costume in a matter of seconds and immediately adopted her calming voice of easy reassurance.

I had witnessed the act before. Mary would ask leading questions to arrive at a place in the woman's life and through balanced acts of listening and caring she'd make a connection.

"People are suffering," she once told me. "They need me to commiserate."

Unbelievably Layla and Mary had visited city hall and obtained a license for their little street endeavor so there was little chance that the cops would stop the show. As Mary got started with her first customer a line formed.

"This never ceases to amaze me," I said to Layla.

Layla didn't bother to answer. It was as if I hadn't spoken. I wrote it off as her being interested in Mary's taking apart the life of Ellen, her first customer. It seemed that Ellen's husband had stepped out on her and was more interested in the new girlfriend than the old wife.

"Will he come back to me?" Ellen asked in tears.

Madame Marie had obtained that information within three minutes of shaking Ellen's hand.

"Let's see what the cards say," Mary said.

"You can't trust men," Layla said under her breath. "They'll pretend they love you and then they'll secretly text their ex-girlfriends behind your back."

"Le Chariot," Mary said. "You have to accept that your partner is different from you. If you love him, take him with his faults and virtues. Give him time and space to be himself. He will be faithful and loyal and honest if you don't suffocate him with your lack of confidence. If you change, your relationship will improve."

Ellen was nodding along. What Layla had said was seeping into my tiny brain. I reached for her.

"Leave me the fuck alone," Layla said through gritted teeth. "Just take Rachael back. I don't need your shit."

Mary was hugging Ellen goodbye. The two women had made a bright connection in just a few minutes time. I was certain that Ellen's heart felt better but mine felt as if it were in a vice. I didn't have much of a chance to go over all of it with Layla, but it was obvious that she'd read my texts to Rachael.

"Next in line," Layla said as she accepted another ten-dollar bill. "We'll talk later, traitor," she whispered to me. Madame Marie shook hands with Earl, a young black college student who wanted to know about love.

"The tower!" Madame Marie exclaimed. "You are afraid, but this is normal because you know that you need a radical change in your life. You need a metamorphosis to fill you with energy, to help you fight against the monotony and boredom of loneliness. This is a period of spiritual renovation, seduction, well-being and improvement. Now you will be able to start a serious, passionate relationship."

Mary's words bit into me and Earl at the exact same moment. Layla also caught the connection, turning to snarl at me as Madame Marie and Earl hugged for a long moment. I simply walked away.

Was it possible to love Layla? Did she want me to? She was twenty-something years younger than me, but Mary's reading of the card brought a few things to light. I was lonely and Layla was lonely, and we both needed a metamorphosis, but what if we crashed and burned?

I headed to the place where I'd last seen Adam and Rolando. I needed to check in on that problem as well. My heart ached, but two squealing teenage girls stopped me dead in my tracks. We were mere feet from the front entrance to the arena. The girls were teenage Springsteen fans and it occurred to me that they hadn't even been born when *Tunnel of Love* was released.

"I shook Bruce's hand!" the girl shouted. She was dressed all in black. A *Born in the USA* button was on her right lapel.

"What?" I asked.

"Bruce and Nils were just here," she said. "Two security guards were blocking the door, but Bruce and Nils walked right past them without even looking up. I walked right up to Bruce, told him I loved him, and just before I passed out he said, *Hello Sweetheart*."

The girl let out another blood-curdling scream.

"You gotta' be kidding me, where'd they go?"

"They got into a black Ford Explorer and drove away," the girl said. "Bruce was driving. Oh my God! I can die now!"

It was exactly what I might say. I looked in the direction of where the girl had pointed at the Explorer driving away.

"How long ago was this?" I asked.

"Three minutes," she said. "You missed seeing him by three minutes!"

Perfect. Just fucking perfect.

***

Adam wasn't much of a barber, but I had to admit that when he was done with Rolando I hardly recognized my friend. The two of them were three sheets to the wind by four in the afternoon, however, and when I found them sitting on the back tailgate of the truck there were a mountain of beer cans at their feet.

"Your father did the right thing," Rolando said. "You didn't even know that broad in Omaha. Can you imagine what might have happened ten years from now? I've watched people live in total hate of one another for the sake of the fucking kids and they end up torturing the kids and each other."

If Rolando was worried about being busted by the cops he was doing a good job of hiding it. I leaned to the case and plucked a beer out. I twisted the tab and took a hearty gulp.

"How goes the carnival show?" Rolando asked.

"They were ten deep in line when I left," I said. "Mary's a wonder of the world."

Rolando laughed a bit too loudly.

"I never doubted it for a second," Adam said.

Rolando moved his ass so I'd have a corner of the tailgate to sit on. I raised my beer can in salute.

"What's the story with Layla?" Rolando asked.

I'd been thinking of little else since she growled at me.

"I have no idea," I said. I sipped the beer and had to squint my eyes to avoid the sun that was riding high.

"I once had a dog that loved me like she loves you," Rolando said. "It's strange but I acted a lot like you're acting. I appreciated that dog's love but I was real scared of fucking her."

Adam and Rolando high-fived. They laughed loud enough to attract a bit of attention by people walking along the newly configured waterfront.

"What am I supposed to do?" I asked.

"I told you before, buddy," Adam said. "Hold onto all of the love you can find."

I finished my beer and headed back to the fortune-tellers booth. I felt less confused in the land of spirituality than I did in Rolando's world. They were right though, I had to make up with Layla.

"I can't believe that bitch shook Bruce's hand." I roared to the sky once I got out of Adam and Rolando's earshot.

***

The anticipation of the moment when Bruce and the band walk on stage is worth the price of admission. Since we were in great seats, a mere hundred feet or so from the stage, we watched the band members taking their places, in the dark. When Bruce bounded up the stairs to the stage Mary turned to me with tears in her eyes.

"He's here!" she shouted.

"He better fucking *be* here," Rolando answered.

The first musical notes of the night hit my ears and the surge of excitement turned my entire body into a quivering mess. We heard the unmistakable opening.

"Oh my God!!! *Badlands!*" Mary screamed. For the first time of the night we hugged. We'd repeat the ritual through twenty-six songs.

I was seated between Mary and Rolando. Adam and Layla were on the other side of Mary, and it was sickening to me, but I wasn't getting any of Layla's reaction to what she was seeing on the stage. Until the band geared up and played *Out in the Street.*

Layla was singing along. The tears that I'd seen racing down Mary's face looked even lovelier as they traced a path down Layla's smooth skin. She leaned across Adam and around Mary and brought me in for a hug.

"I *do* love you, stupid," she said.

Halfway through the show my cell phone buzzed. I glanced down to see the text message left by Anna.

"Hi Joseph," it read. "It's my turn to leave you a message and a word of the day."

Bruce was at center stage getting ready to drift into the crowd as he sang loud and clear about waiting for the sun to pierce the clouds.

I turned to gauge the reaction of the crowd. The lights were up; there were thousands of anonymous people standing on their seats, pumping their fists high into the air. My body was electrified as every single cell jumped to be heard.

"Our quote of the day is from Lord Byron," Anna's text read. "*To have joy, one must share it. Happiness was born a twin.*"

I couldn't help myself. Bruce was holding the microphone out for a boy of about eight. The kid was singing the chorus. I was crying. I felt Rolando's tap on my left shoulder.

"You're a big fucking baby!" he shouted over the crowd.

I glanced back down to the text.

"Our word of the day is *orchestrated*," Anna wrote. "God's love for us is orchestrated and undying."

Rolando clasped me on the back as Bruce slowed it down and began the song that Rolando had come to see, *Thunder Road*. When Bruce got to the line that summed up all of Rolando's days up to that point it was my turn to shout at him.

"Who's the fucking baby now?"

"I love you, Joseph," Anna's text read. "But don't worry about me so much. We're doing good now. You helped me be the best.

Thank you."

I tapped Adam and Mary on the shoulder and immediately bridged the gap between me and Layla. By the time *Born to Run* started and the crowd reached an even higher fever I was fully wrapped in Layla's arms.

"I love you too," I cried.

Chapter 15 – Dreams and Visions

The parking lot had long since cleared out. The band had played for just a little over three hours. We walked the area around the arena for the next two hours, hoping beyond hope that we'd see the members of the E Street Band getting into the back of the bus or a black Explorer for their ride across town.

"What hotel do you think they're staying in?" Layla asked. Her voice was barely audible as she'd shouted herself hoarse.

"You can bet your ass he isn't sleeping on the floor of the Econo-Lodge," Rolando said. I noticed that Rolando's voice was also a bit worse for the wear.

"Mother-fucker is sixty-two years old," Rolando said. "Did you see him chug the beer that someone handed him out of the crowd?"

"You can probably drink more beer than him," Adam said.

"No doubt."

We never even saw the approach of the police car. The searchlight was on us before we could even gather our senses.

"Time to clear out!" the first officer out of the car shouted.

I couldn't help but think that he'd instantly recognize Rolando who was now dressed as a Springsteen roadie with an E Street Band baseball cap and a *Born to Run* tee-shirt that showed Bruce and Clarence standing back-to-back.

"Are we drinking and driving our way out of here tonight?" A second officer asked. He looked a little like Tom Selleck and I think I heard Mary purr beside me. She was also aware of our problem with Rolando so she took immediate charge.

"I don't drink at all," she said to the officer. "We were just moving out. The show was absolutely electric."

"The guy's a dinosaur," the younger officer said. I saw him steal a glance at Layla, who had returned to her spot on my right side. "But people seem to love him."

Rolando had escaped to the back of the car. Thankfully we had put the last of the beer away and I worked to clean our mess as the officers listened to Mary's mad recap of the love we had all shared.

"Drive safe," Tom Selleck said. "The highway's jammed with broken heroes."   We all laughed. Most importantly, we were on our way out of town with our dreams still intact.

"Pittsburgh here we come!" Adam shouted.

***

The microphone was alive on that trip West on I-90. Mary was driving the first leg, but she left Layla with specific instructions about what came next.

"Madame Marie not only helped 45 people tonight she took ten dollars of their hard-earned money. We now have just fewer than five-hundred dollars in the grey box, and we'd have almost six hundred if we didn't have to buy Rolando and Adam a thirty-pack of beer every twenty minutes."

Rolando raised his beer can high. "Fucking eh-right!" he shouted.

"Bruce was fantastic, right people?" Layla shouted through the mic. "Have we all been effectively Bruced?"

"Bruced?" Rolando asked. "He's a fucking verb now?"

Layla's laugh was wonderful. She tilted her head back and flicked her golden hair back off her shoulder.

"He is one sexy old man, isn't he?" she shouted. She danced in the aisle as if she could still hear the chorus of *Out in the Street*.

"The message of Bruce and the band is clear," she said. "Live life. Don't give into the fear. Trust God and love, love, love, love! That's what getting Bruced means."

On cue Adam turned the stereo up loud as the opening chords of *Working On a Dream* filled the air.

"Wait! Wait! Wait!" Layla yelled. "I have a couple of more announcements!"

Adam turned the volume down. Rolando handed Adam a beer across the aisle.

"Pittsburgh is a great city," Layla cried out. "We have perfect seats once more, and while, thanks to our fortune teller, money isn't as big of a problem, we are going to earn more. Tonight we have reservations at the Comfort Inn. We were able to spring for two rooms. Mary and Adam will be in room one and Rolando, Joseph and me will share the other. Everyone gets a bed!"

Rolando clapped his hands in a maniacal manner. "Are you bunking with me?" he shouted to Layla.

"I'll be sharing my bed with Joseph," Layla said with a curtsy.

Adam returned his attention back to the stereo, but Layla stopped him once more.

"There's more," she said. "Tomorrow afternoon we're entered in a karaoke contest at a happening bar in Pittsburgh. We called ahead to save our spots at the Buckhead Saloon. There are cash prizes for the top three acts and we figure to be a shoe-in for the five-hundred dollar first prize with Adam as Bruce and Joseph as Little Steven. I'll play Patty and Mary will be Suzie Tyrell because she can actually play the violin. We're even toying with the idea of dressing Rolando up as Clarence."

Layla's wonderful laugh filled the air once more.

"I'm playing the fucking dead guy?" Rolando asked.

As the laughter filled the inside of the van I thought of all that had happened in just a couple of week's time. Since the moment Rachael and Anna had walked out the door I'd been dying little by little, piece by piece. It felt so good to come back to life in the company of friends that I actually loved. I met Layla at the front of the bus. Without thinking too much about it I kissed her as passionately as I'd ever kissed anyone. The cheer that went up was as worthy as any cheer that Bruce had generated at the show.

"Cue the music!" I yelled to Adam.

I sang the opening line of that song as if my life depended on it. I was working on a dream too.

***

About six hours later, as the sun began to climb in the early morning sky, I shared the queen-sized bed with Layla. Rolando's wall-shaking snoring had found a bit of a rhythm about three hours earlier. The big man had fallen asleep as his head was on the way to the pillow and we weren't very concerned about waking him as he'd finished at least twenty beers on the trip.

"I don't care that you're older than me," Layla whispered. "I don't care that we look like an odd couple. It's your heart that I love, Joseph."

Her words came to my ears as if they were part of one of my long-standing daydreams. Her soft lips on mine were beyond comprehension. Her perfect, young body was pressed tightly to mine and the ache of desire was particularly mind-blowing. Deep in the recesses of my heart there was enough doubt to sink a ship, but for those hours as we kissed and touched one another I held them at bay.

"It's not about us," I whispered back. "That's not what scares me. It's Anna. How do I let Anna go?"

"You don't have to let her go," Layla said. "Didn't you learn anything tonight at the concert?"

I was a little perplexed by the question.

"You've been chasing your life around since day one," she said. "When everything you need to live is right there inside your heart, and right here in front of you. You keep waiting for your ship to come in, and I'm telling you, it's docked."

"How did you arrive at all this so soon?" I asked.

"I knew it the minute I heard Mary talking to you at that restaurant on the day I met you," she said. "The part of me that my step-father tried to kill came alive at that moment."

Our lips met once more and as our tongues wrestled for position it became quite apparent to me that Rolando's snoring had ceased.

I'm not sure what made me do it at that exact moment but I bolted upright causing Layla to nearly fall off the bed. As I'd suspected, Rolando was wide awake. He was sitting on the edge of his bed a mere foot away from where we'd held our embrace.

"Don't let me interrupt," he said in full voice. "I'm really looking forward to the moment when you two finally bump uglies."

I threw a pillow that struck Rolando in the face.

"Seriously, you two are the best," he said. "I hope you're together for the next eighty years."

Rolando left the bed, throwing the pillow back at my head.

"Here's the plan," he said. "I'm going into the bathroom to shit, shower and shave. I figure to take about a half an hour. By the time I get back you two better have consummated this relationship, or I swear to God, Joseph, I'm gonna do it for you."

Layla was laughing a joyful laugh that could have been set to music.

"The dogs on Main Street howl," Rolando sang out in full voice.

Shortly after he closed the bathroom door the door to a brand new universe opened for me.

"I'll love you forever," Layla cried when we were done. "We can be as happy as we make up our minds to be."

"You're spending too much time with Mary," I said. "But now you're necessary, Layla. I might not make your dreams come true, but I can help."

"That's beautiful," Layla said as a tear escaped the corner of her left eye, and then as if a light bulb went off, she laughed.

"I just got Bruced, didn't I?"

I laughed right along with her. We continued to hold one another tight right up until the moment when we heard the rustling around the bathroom and Rolando's booming approach. By the end of our little session I was as happy as I'd ever been, and I was still scared to death.

***

The Buckhead Saloon was actually a bit hard for us to find right out of the shoot.

"It's on White Station Square Drive," Mary announced into the microphone as Adam negotiated the truck along a one-way street.

"We passed it," Layla called out.

"I know we passed it," Adam barked, "I couldn't get in the left lane."

My head was pounding a bit. The ringing in my ears took a while to subside from the show, and my back ached a bit from standing for three hours, and then giving up sleep to make love to Layla. Yet there was no mistaking what was happening to me. I was absolutely, one-hundred percent alive. There wasn't much that could happen to change that. My cell phone vibrated as Adam finally was able to make the left onto White Station Square Drive. The number on the screen was unrecognizable, but was from the Buffalo area.

"Hello?"

"Joseph!"

Anna's voice was like music in my ear.

"We're in Buffalo."

My heart rose and sunk at the same time, and the pressure in my chest was instantaneous.

"Buffalo?" I asked. "Why are you in Buffalo, beautiful?"

We had pulled into the parking lot of the bar. Layla's left hand was on the inside of my right thigh. She leaned in close. I covered the phone and mouthed the word, 'Anna.' Layla neither smiled nor frowned. We were both undeniably caught between elation and misery.

"Grandma is in the hospital," Anna said. "We had to come home."

Anna sounded as if she were on the verge of tears.

"But I can't wait to see you," Anna added in a voice that was quivering with excitement.

Layla was wearing a Springsteen shirt from the Buffalo show that was powder blue and featured a set of wings around Bruce's name as if angels were carrying the letters to a higher ground.

"Are you coming over?" Anna asked.

"We've arrived," Rolando called out. "Hang up the fucking phone."

"Who's that?" Anna asked.

All at once the ringing in my ears was way more pronounced. My tongue felt too big for my mouth. I thought of the nights when I'd hold Anna close and sing the words to Bruce's most famous song, *Born to Run*. I had changed the name of the character in the song from Wendy to Anna.

Layla's eyes were pleading with me to get off the bus and follow her down the steps. Anna's voice was talking excitedly in my ear. The push and pull and the Springsteen verse were all competing for time in my head, and the last thing I remember before hitting the floor was pitching straight forward in despair.

I came to in the parking lot of the Buckhead Saloon. The first set of eyes I saw were those belonging to Mary. They were upside down.

Mary held my head in her lap as she sat in the gravel lot. She was holding a warm washcloth to my pounding head.

"What the fuck?" I asked. It was actually the perfect question for what was happening around me. Adam, Rolando and Layla were dressing for the karaoke contest.

"You passed out," Mary whispered.

Rolando ripped the sleeves off the black shirt that Adam was wearing. Layla worked to tie a bright red bandana around Adam's head.

"Anna," I whispered, remembering that I had been on the phone.

"Shhhhh," Mary whispered. "I spoke to her for you, and to Rachael."

"I have to get back to Buffalo," I said. I tried to rise up, but Mary showed surprising strength in holding me down.

"I'm only gonna' say this once," Mary said. "You know I love you as much as I love myself."

My head was threatening to explode and I felt the tears in my eyes. Mary wiped them away with a soft touch.

"Your life is now," she said. "It's what you see right here, dancing in front of you. I'm not saying that there's not room for Anna and Rachael, somewhere down the line, but right there," Anna said as she pointed to Rolando and Layla fighting over the correct way to tie the bandana around Adam's head. "Right there is love. Your head is in the lap of a woman who would die for you. Joseph, with all my heart, I beg you not to press the issue. Stand straight up, put on your Little Steven costume and come into that bar with us."

Mary tried hard to catch every single one of the tears that were racing down my face.

"Anna was worried about you, but I talked to her. I gave her the quote for the day from William James. It was the quote I'd saved for you today, *Believe that life is worth living, and your belief will help create the fact.*"

Mary was stroking my head as if I was a newborn child and she was a first-time mother.

"Our word for the day is *palladium.* I explained to Anna that palladium means anything that is believed to provide protection or safety. I told her that you'd always be there to safeguard her love."

The red bandana was finally tied perfectly around Adam's head and my tears gave way to a sudden burst of laughter as I realized that he looked exactly as Bruce had looked in 1983. Rolando was also a spitting image of the Clarence with the obvious difference being that he was a white big man.

"How did we get to this point?" I asked Mary.

"Love," she said. "And someday we'll get to the point where we can walk with our heads held high."

Of course, I could finish the thought for her.

"Until then, *tramps like us,*" I said.

Mary, with Rolando's help, got me to my feet. The sun peeked out from behind a cloud just above the sign advertising the Buckhead Saloon. Who knew that life would truly begin for me in Pittsburgh-fucking-Pennsylvania?

***

Adam was simply brilliant. He danced, gyrated and shimmied his way across the stage in the saloon that was home to two massive bars and a crowded dance floor, in a ski-lodge-themed building. When Adam was on the stage belting out the chorus to *Born in the USA* the men set down their pool cues and watched. Rolando mimed a perfect Clarence sax solo during our rendition of *Jungleland* and I did my best to portray a gangster as Little Steven. We won the five hundred dollar prize without a single vote even having to be cast. At the bar we basked in our triumph. Adam's arm was around my shoulder.

"You all right, dude?" He screamed.

I raised my shot glass filled with Jameson's Irish whiskey and stole a glance at Layla who, while talking with Rolando, tossed her head back in pure joy as she laughed.

"Never better," I said. "But just so you know *Born in the USA* isn't a happy song. When you sing the part about the soldier in Viet Nam with the woman he loved you should remember that the soldier died. You were up there shaking your hips in a humping motion!"

Adam laughed. We downed the shots.

"Bruce also said something about it not being a sin to be glad you're alive, or some shit," Adam said.

CHAPTER 16 –ONE STEP UP

After the third concert in less than a week we boarded the truck on an unbelievable high. The E Street Band had ripped through all of our favorite songs. For Layla, *Out in the Street* was the fourth song. Mary was thrilled with the rendition of *The Rising*, and she actually laughed when Bruce mentioned Ralph in a raucous version of *Johnny 99*. Adam did his best Bruce shake in *Dancing in the Dark*, and Rolando and I high-fived every single time Bruce sang the line about the howling dogs on Main Street. Rolando also screamed at the top of his lungs when Bruce mentioned that he didn't want to be alone again in the encore during the sing-along that was *Thunder Road*.

There was just one thing missing: we were on this tour thinking that we would eventually have to shake Bruce's hand to make all that we were going through stand up. We tried to work our way back stage, but the security guards blocked us at every turn.

As we waited in the parking lot to escape the arena we talked it out.

"We need a plan," Mary croaked into the microphone. "We are about halfway through and we haven't got near one member of the

177

band."

"What about his publicity team?" Adam asked. "Can't we tell them a story that will get Bruce in the middle of us? Lord knows we have enough sadness. Bruce is a prophet. His job is to take away our sadness."

"Why don't you just get your old man to hire the band for an hour?" Rolando asked.

Eventually the talk died out. We had the second longest stretch of highway of the entire trip to cover. Layla was behind the wheel for the first couple of hours from Pittsburgh to Toronto and the plan was for me to take over in Erie. I would cover the distance from Erie to Buffalo where we would stop, once more, to visit with Rachael and Anna before heading north of the border.

Mary took a moment to go over our financials again.

"We're spending too much money on shirts, hats and beer," she said. "After we fill up the truck we'll be down under three hundred dollars again."

"How in the hell did that happen?" Adam asked.

"The concert shirts are forty bucks a pop," Mary said. "We bought five more there, and we spent over a hundred dollars at the concession stand. It's Joseph's turn to raise a bit of money so think about it, buddy."

"We aren't cutting the beer allowance," Rolando said as he popped the tab on an iced cold Budweiser. As he did so, he motioned me to the seat beside him. I crossed the aisle and sat down next to Rolando as he raised the beer high and then emptied half of it in a single gulp. Mary frowned as Rolando broke her rule about drinking while the truck was moving, but she let him drink the beer.

"Can you help me with something?" Rolando whispered in the dark of the back of the truck.

"Sure," I said.

"I didn't even tell you what it is," he said. He paused for a long while. "You're a good dude, Joseph."

I waited for Rolando to speak, but he just sat there for a long moment staring at the beer can. He was definitely trying to piece it all together in his mind.

"I need help," he said. "When this is all over with, I need help."

"Anything," I said.

Rolando smiled again.

"It's been a hard life," he said. "From day one I've been kind of fucked, you know?"

"I know," I whispered. "Me too."

"And I've been looking at it all wrong," Rolando said. "I've tried to tear myself apart at every single turn. I've had my own sense of justice that's sort of screwed me time after time. They're gonna' eventually arrest me for beating the hell out of Ralph, but Mary didn't deserve that, right? Still, it's gonna' ruin me again."

I had no idea what I should be saying, but I've lived long enough to know that sometimes the best thing to do is listen.

"I went to college for two weeks," Rolando said. "I had a teacher there who read the lesson straight out of the book. Every day for the first half an hour he'd read us the damn book and then ask us the questions at the back. I called him on it. I told him that he should be teaching it to us instead of just puking up what someone else had written. He threw me out of his class, and I quit. I was too stupid to just sit there and shut up, and I never went back."

Rolando sipped his beer again and burped loudly.

"I had a girl too, Heather. Man, she was as pretty as Layla. When I left college she got fed up with me. I didn't have a job, a dime, a family, or a future, and she wondered why I would just bag it and get wasted. She married a fucking guy who works at a bank. They got three kids and a real nice house out in the country. The last time I ran into her, at a grocery store of all places, she looked at me real strange, you know? You know what she was thinking?"

"No," I said.

"She was thinking that I'm pitiful."

"You aren't pitiful," I said.

Rolando laughed. "The fuck I ain't. I gained a hundred pounds. I get drunk or high every fucking day. I bet horses. I eat shit. I didn't have a friend in the world until you invited me on this trip, and every damn thing I've ever done has blown up in my stupid face. I'm not a loser, but I sure as hell know how to live like one."

Rolando crumpled the beer can. The rest of the truck was quiet. Adam and Mary were sleeping side-by-side under a huge blanket. Beautiful Layla was staring straight out at the yellow line in the center of the highway. The music was Bruce, of course, but it was *The Ghost of Tom Joad* CD and it was on low.

"You asked me for help," I whispered. "What can I do?"

"Two things," Rolando said. "First, get me all of the Bruce lyrics, would you? He has a message for me, and I'm feeling it."

"That's easy enough," I said.

"Well, there's actually three things," Rolando said. "I need another beer."

I reached across the seat and retrieved two beers out of the ice.

"The first two were easy," I said. "What's number three?"

"Don't leave me alone again," Rolando said. "I don't wanna' be alone."

"Done deal," I said. We tapped cans, and as Layla drove us forward, it occurred to me, once more, that the promised land was our ultimate goal, whether we shook hands with Bruce or not.

By the time we arrived in Erie we were all thankful for the opportunity to stretch our legs. I was also starving and needed at least three cups of coffee. Layla angled the truck into a tight parking spot at the front entrance to a Denny's Restaurant.

"I've got news," Mary said as she skipped off the bus and held the door open for all of us to enter. "I just talked to Ralph. He dropped the charges against Rolando."

I stepped dead in my tracks.

"In exchange for what?" I asked. "You didn't agree to see him again, did you?"

Mary's eyes headed straight for the small carpet just inside the front door.

"That isn't happening," Adam said behind me. "We'd rather stand by Rolando if he's charged than send you back with that son-of-a-bitch."

We had all stopped just inside the front door. There were eight probing eyes centered on Mary.

"I only agreed to talk to him," she said. "He's talking about going into rehab. I've loved him for a long time. Sometimes it's not easy to just blast your way out of the negative vortex."

"That's fucking bullshit," Rolando said.

His words drifted across the floor of the restaurant and a number of heads were raised up off their plates of eggs.

"We'll talk about it later," Layla whispered. "There are five of us," she said to the approaching waitress.

As we approached the table the angst of just plain living was ringing in my ears as loudly as the music had at the concert. It seemed that we all were real adept at getting into our own way. We were content to forever take one step up and two steps back.

Three of us ordered the grand slam breakfast. Before the meal was even delivered Rolando had conned Adam and me out of our bacon.

"So Joseph, you've had some time to think. How are we going to make our money for the Canadian portion of our trip?"

I really didn't have any good ideas, but the idea that Rolando might hit a lucky streak was winning the battle of wits.

"The Seneca-Niagara Casino," I said. "We're going gambling."

"So, the itinerary is a stop in Buffalo, correct? We are going to meet up with Rachael and Anna, right?" Mary asked.

I nodded through another long sip of coffee. I was trying to show everyone that I'd be able to handle such a visit without being conflicted and I squeezed Layla's hand under the table as I did so.

"Rachael suggested we meet up at the Anchor Bar and have a few chicken wings. She swears that we won't be speaking about anything too heavy because Anna will be there."

As I said her name my heart swelled a bit. I was on my way to see beautiful Anna.

"I need some time," Adam said. "Before we leave here I'm going to need an hour or so to make a few phone calls. I have an idea for my father, and it really can't wait."

Adam's sudden input quieted all of us for a moment, but he didn't offer up anything more.

"Gambling?" Mary asked. "Do you think we can win? Because the thing about gambling is that we could just as easily lose everything."

"We're fucking gambling," Rolando said. "We did your little rain dance when we all thought it was pointless so get with the flow, Madame Marie."

The waitress refilled our coffee cups as Mary produced the gray box. She rifled through the cash we had left and before she closed the box Layla grabbed the show tickets for the Toronto and New Jersey concerts and eyed them hungrily.

"The best part about it is that we get to see Bruce four more times."

We all agreed.

Layla studied the tickets for a few more moments, and then we all got up from the table and headed back to the truck. We were shuffling off to Buffalo once more.

***

As I drove I noticed that our group was becoming a bit more serious about things. Mary was sitting beside Rolando and they were talking non-stop with wild gesturing eyes and long bouts of laughter. Adam was alone in the back, talking incessantly on his cell phone. Layla was caught up in the scenery flying by as we covered the ground from Erie to downtown Buffalo. Bruce, of course, was along for the ride. I had chosen the *Magic* album to accompany us and I was singing along to *The Last to Die*.

Two hours after leaving the Denny's restaurant in Erie we pulled into the parking lot of the Anchor Bar on Main Street in Buffalo. I was about to see Anna for the first time in a long time and my heart was dancing as I leafed through the rolodex in my mind for just the right quote for her.

Every minute of life comes with it its miraculous value, and its face of eternal youth.

I had plenty to tell Anna. For the first time in my life I was absolutely in love and right on cue Layla found her spot beside me in the parking lot on a bright sunny day. She kissed me on the right cheek as she stretched her arms high above her head. She was wearing a Bruce shirt, of course, and the cover shot of the *Darkness on the Edge of Town* pictured Bruce as a young man. Time passes you by while you're busy waiting for something to happen.

"I love you," Layla said, as she wrapped her arms around my waist.

Just when you think that life can't happen for you, it does. I kissed Layla, dreaming that we were the only two people left in the world, but we weren't. Rachael and Anna pulled into the lot and honked the horn, breaking the embrace.

Anna's door flung open and she ran to me. She was as perfect as I imagined her to be. She jumped and I gobbled her up into my arms as both Rachael and Layla stood side-by-side watching pure love in action.

"I missed you so much," I whispered into Anna's left ear. Her golden hair was waving in the wind and when I leaned her back to take in the sight of her perfect face I noticed the tears.

"We're moving back here," she said. "Who's that?"

I lowered Anna to the ground.

"This is my girlfriend, Layla," I said. "We met while you were out in California and we really love each other."

I had never been anything but honest with Anna, or even Rachael for that matter. I didn't see that there was any other way to handle the introduction, and I owed that much to Layla because I did love her.

Anna looked confused for a split-second but then her eyes grew wide with happiness.

"You deserve to be in love," she said.

Despite the fact that we'd all had a big breakfast, twenty minutes later the waiter delivered thirty medium and thirty hot chicken wings to the table. The Anchor Bar was the first restaurant to serve chicken wings in such a manner and the story of the dish was written on the placemats. The owners, Frank and Theresa, had discovered a world famous dish by mistake. There was steam rising from the wings and we passed the plates around, smiling non-stop, and chatting incessantly about the trip that we were on. I sat beside Rachael and Anna and across from Layla. Could it all possibly be this easy? Would love allow us to make it through without so much as a cross word of jealousy of competition? I was still way too nervous to comprehend it all, but it was Mary and Rolando who provided the balance.

"You want to see a magic trick?" Mary asked. She produced a deck of cards and even the simple act of shuffling captured all of us as Mary spoke softly. Anna was enraptured by Mary's hand movements and I took a moment to turn to Rachael.

"It didn't work out?" I whispered.

"He wasn't really interested in us," Rachael said. Her eyes flashed across the table at Layla, and then back to me. "Anna's right, by the way," Rachael said. "You do deserve love. We'll find our way. Just promise me that you'll be around for us once in awhile."

"Of course," I whispered.

"She's kind of young," Rachael said. It wasn't an accusation, but there was a degree of pain on Rachael's tired face.

"Yeah, it's something," I said.

"No way!!!" Anna screamed as Mary produced her card. "How did you do that?"

It took us over an hour to finish off our lunch. When the check came Rolando pulled out the grey box and reached for it, but Rachael's hand came down on top of his.

"I got it," Rachael said.

"I ain't arguing with you," Rolando said. "We need beer money in Toronto."

Rolando had opened and closed the box, but I watched his expression change, and he opened the box again as Rachael was mentally figuring the tip. Rolando cleared his throat.

"I don't mean to be a Debby downer here, but where the fuck are the tickets?" Rolando clasped his hand over his mouth when it registered that Anna was within earshot.

Layla grabbed the box from Rolando and her face turned pink as she sifted through the cash. There were instant tears in her eyes.

"I never put them back," she said. "I left them on the table at Denny's."

The silence around the table was absolutely deafening. Layla had left behind two thousand dollars worth of Bruce tickets.

Like a shot Mary was out of her seat and by Layla's side. I realized that comforting Layla was probably my job but I was too stunned to move. Rolando's fury grew before my eyes, but he held his tongue.

"Maybe Adam has them," Mary said.

"Where the hell is he?" Rolando asked.

We had been all too busy eating lunch to realize that Adam was gone.

"I'm not sure," I said. "He was on the phone all morning and he never came in."

I was a little suspicious of Adam's activity. He had let us all down before. Perhaps there was a woman lurking in the shadows, or he was having more trouble with his father. In any regard his sudden disappearance was disturbing.

"The truck is gone," Rolando said after glancing out the side window to the spot where it should have been parked.

"I'll call his phone," Mary said and then a moment later. "It went straight to voice mail."

Anna went to Layla's side. She too was offering the comfort that I should have been offering, but I was too stunned. What did I think was going to happen? Every single time it appeared that life was about to break my way something came along to shit all over it. We didn't have tickets and Adam was gone. Layla was broken-hearted and I was just sitting there, again.

We stood in the parking lot for over an hour. I spent most of that time pacing back and forth and silently cursing Adam, Layla, and the moon above. Was our trip suddenly over? Would I be able to forgive and forget Layla for losing the tickets? It was just before Adam turned into the back lot with the tires squealing that Anna put it all in perspective for each one of us.

"Old people are so weird," she said. "You get all worked up over nothing. It's a beautiful day, we're all happy, and things will work out. Why isn't that enough?"

Indeed. Why didn't we ever feel as if we had enough in life?

"Most people aren't happy unless they're miserable," Mary said.

Adam's screeching tires had brought the thought to a halt.

"Toronto!" Adam yelled out the open side window.

"One problem," Rolando yelled back. "Lindsey Lohan lost the tickets."

Despite our predicament we all laughed, even Layla.

"No biggie," Adam said. "I have insurance on them through American Express, we're golden."

I hugged Layla tightly and tears of gratitude filled her perfect eyes. She kissed me flush on the mouth as Anna and Rachael took in the scene. It was at that moment that I realized that despite my glee I was about to say goodbye to them again.

"Give me a minute," I said.

Rachael, Anna and I moved a few steps clear of the truck. We'd spent all that time playing house, and even though we had no idea what was next, we were together again.

"I have the quote and the word of the day," Anna said excitedly. "I've been saving them for you."

I opened my arms and Anna jumped into them.

"*Success is a journey, not a destination*," she said. "Some guy named Ben Sweetland said that."

"That's a great one," I said.

"And you're a *mensch*," she said. "That means you're a decent, upright, responsible person."

"You're a mensch," I said.

I kissed her on both cheeks and then the lips. I wasn't fast enough to tell her that I loved her first.

"Talk to Mom," Anna whispered into my right ear.

I set Anna on the ground and she drifted away. I caught Rolando's eye peering out at me from the back window of the truck. I didn't want to rush anything, and to Rolando's credit, he was being patient. Rachael took two steps to me as Anna drifted away from us.

"I love you too," Rachael said. "And I know we're gonna' all be all right."

"Probably not," I said, and we both laughed.

"My word of the day is *obtuse*," Rachael said. "That means not quick or alert in perception, feeling or intellect. Sometimes I'm obtuse, but the universe will provide."

"You sound like Mary," I said. "And your quote?"

"Old Chinese proverb," Rachael said. "*Be not afraid of growing slowly. Be afraid, only, of standing still.*"

We hugged for a long moment and I repeated the kiss sequence on Rachael's pretty face. Suddenly I had an idea.

"Why don't you come with us?" I asked. "Maybe Bruce will bring Anna up on stage to sing or dance with him."

"Not this time," Rachael said. "But someday you might get me to see him."

I watched Anna's eyes drift to the truck and settle in on Layla.

"She's young," Rachael said. "But she's perfect for you, I never saw you so happy, Joseph. So, *Joe, I gotta' go. We had it once, we ain't got it anymore.*"

We both laughed.

"You have to stop saying that," I said.

"You'll never really get rid of me, Joseph," Rachael said. "You may see me a lot sooner than you think."

"I hope so," I said.

We had finally tested Rolando's patience. He wanted to get the show on the road and he told us of this by lowering the window and belching loudly.

"After supper motherfuckers," He screamed out. "Let's make like a fetus and head out."

It was the perfect ending for such a scene as instead of crying we all laughed.

We were ready to chase Bruce across the border, and my heart never felt lighter.

CHAPTER 17 –A LUCKY MAN

The Seneca Niagara Casino is located just a few blocks away from one of the world's wonders, but instead of spending more than a glancing moment at Niagara Falls we headed straight to the gambling den. Mary, of course, wasn't happy with the decision as she definitely preferred staring at the rushing water, but we needed money.

"Everyone gets sixty dollars to gamble," Adam said as he opened the grey box and doled it out. "I don't have to tell you what's at stake. We're either going to sleep in the truck tonight, or we are going to high-roll it at the Marriot after the show."

The mammoth casino lurked in the background as we stood in the parking lot surveying the decay of the city streets of Niagara Falls.

"Isn't it something?" Rolando asked waving at the broken down and abandoned homes. "You have Niagara Falls right over there and the glimmer of the casino and all around is bullshit. This is what Bruce is singing about. We're amusing ourselves to fucking death. It's like life too. A couple of good moments surrounded by a bunch of shit."

The fact that Rolando was saying such a thing wasn't lost on any of us. He'd grown more on this trip than all the rest of us combined.

We entered the casino from the parking ramp area. The hundreds and hundreds of slot machines beckoned to all of us, but we would all be on individual trips to the place.

"We only need one of us to win," Mary said. "Spend your sixty bucks wisely. We meet at the bar in the lobby in one hour."

We put our hands in the center as if we were breaking the huddle at a football game. We'd head off on separate paths with one common goal in mind.

"Win!" We called out.

I couldn't have lost my money any faster than I did. Layla was beside me as I put my three twenty's into a dollar slot machine and hit the button for maximum bet. It didn't take us long to count back from sixty-to-zero, three bucks at a time.

"Wow, that was fun," Layla said.

The entire episode had taken just over six minutes. As much as I wanted to be a winner, I just wasn't.

"You bet too much," Layla said. "Let's try the penny machines with my share."

I sat beside her with my hand on her thigh as she hit the button and cried out in excitement when she won eleven dollars on one spin. Eventually though we found our way straight to zero.

"Broke," Layla said as the last spin came up empty. We had 24 minutes left before we were to meet the others.

"Now what?" she asked.

"I don't know," I said.

The broken down old man seated to my right was leaning across, playing two machines at once. One of the machines hit for two hundred dollars and the man did not react in the least. He just kept hitting the buttons.

"What's gonna' happen with us?" Layla asked.

It was a fairly open-ended question. Was she talking about being broke and not finishing the trip, or was she asking about our love and how that might crash and burn too?

She grabbed hold of both of my hands and placed them in her lap. We were sitting in front of two machines that we didn't have the money to play.

"I've been thinking a lot," she said. "I want to be your wife."

I almost fell off the chair. The lights and bells seemed suddenly louder as the slot machines buzzed all around me. Was it all a losing gamble? I was suddenly dizzy.

"Oh God, you're gonna' pass out again," Layla said with a melodic laugh. "Come on."

She pulled me to my feet and we escaped the bells and whistles and those who were celebrating and those who were dejected. We had lost everything, couldn't buy a cup of coffee if we pooled our money, and yet we were planning our future.

A hundred feet from the café and thirty feet from the busy restrooms we found a corner of the casino floor that wasn't occupied. Layla pushed my back up against the wall and ground her hips into my hips.

"Do you want to marry me, Joseph?" she asked.

"It just doesn't seem real," I said.

A loud cheer erupted across the room as a group of friends realized that they'd just hit a jackpot.

"Because I really want to marry you," she said. "And it's unlike anything I've ever felt in my life. I don't want you to be scared thinking that we aren't that young anymore. I've been through a lot, but I feel like we're knocking on the door to happiness."

"I just got Bruced," I whispered.

"*I'll wait for you and if I should fall behind, wait for me,*" Layla said.

We kissed for a long time in that back corner of the casino. I wasn't real sure if we'd be winners or losers, and in the end I wasn't sure if I were ready for the gamble. After our make-out session we headed to the lobby bar to see if everyone else did as well as we did. As we walked I felt a distance between us. I wondered if I were imaging it.

***

We ran smack dab into Rolando first. He was sipping a Heineken Light and there was an empty shot glass at his left hand. There was a stack of bills in front of him.

"I hit a hand for three-thirty," he said. "Come on, have a drink."

"No shit," I said. "You made enough back for all of us. At least we covered our bets."

"Not if I keep drinking we didn't," Rolando said.

I sat on the stool next to him and Layla plopped down in my lap. Before she settled in Layla leaned over and kissed Rolando on his right cheek.

"What's that for?" Rolando asked.

"Because you're going to be Joseph's best man at our wedding," Layla said. "Have I ever told you how much I love you, Rolando?"

194

"Not since that time we had sex all night," Rolando said and we all laughed.

The bartender was a distinguished looking older man wearing a red vest and a white bowtie. He waited for our laughter to die down before he asked what I'd like.

"Don't order," Adam called out. "We're having champagne."

Adam was holding tight to a fist-filled with cash as he covered the lobby floor in what should be considered a gallop.

"Thirty-eight hundred," he called out.

Mary edged up to our gathering from behind.

"He shouldn't be announcing what he won," she said. "Someone might rob us, but I really love that goofy bastard."

We downed two bottles of champagne in the lobby of the Seneca-Niagara Casino courtesy of Adam's unbelievable skill at stud poker. As we raised our glasses in salute the song that blasted through the speakers behind the bar was enough to show us that we were blessed to be on the trip.

"The god of music," Rolando called out as the opening line of *Glory Days* blared.

***

Three hours before the Toronto concert we were drinking Triple X beer in the parking lot outside the arena. The beer was bitter-tasting and strong, and it led Rolando to this observation about our Canadian neighbors to the North.

"I'd live up here if it weren't for all the fucking 'eh's' and 'a-boots' and this funny freaking monopoly money."

The back of the truck was open and the Springsteen live CD from New York City was blaring in an attempt to drive out the sounds of the Springsteen *Born to Run* blasting from the car parked three spaces down. On our way into the concert hall we all spoke of the song that Bruce might play that would buoy our spirits once more. We hadn't yet given up hope on shaking the man's hand, but just seeing him so many times in such a short span was helping us round into form.

"*The Rising*," Mary said. Whenever I hear that song I think of the possibilities of life despite what threatens to terrorize us.

"*Working on a Dream*," Layla said. "All I want is coming into focus."

Layla gave my hand a little squeeze as we walked together.

I sort of expected Adam's response to be one of the pop songs from the *Born in the USA* album, but he surprised me.

"*Leah*," he said. "Did you ever really listen to that song? The main character wants to live his life on a higher ground surrounded by those he loves."

"I'm starting to worry about you," I said to Adam.

There were hundreds of people filing by us on the way to see the concert. I thought that they may all be searching for answers as well. For the first time ever it occurred to me that answers don't come in the form of songs. It comes from being comfortable in your own skin and finding love.

"*Better Days*," I said. "I hope he sings *Better Days*."

Once more the show was a frenzy of excitement for each and every one of us. Our seats were three rows from the stage in an area where Bruce strolled by on his way to the center stage where he bandied with the crowd and eventually surfed his way back to the main stage. Mary kept diving over the other two rows in her crazed state in an effort to lay a finger on Bruce as he hurried by. A dive at the very end of the show as Bruce toasted Clarence in the middle of *Tenth Avenue Freeze-out* allowed Mary to get her index finger on the soaked vest Bruce was wearing.

"I touched him!" She wailed as she kissed the tip of her finger. "I'll never wash this finger again."

"You might do all kinds of things with that finger," Rolando said to great laughter.

Once more we waited out the crowd in the parking lot. My voice was hoarse from screaming and Layla's hand was resting comfortably in my own.

"What was your favorite part?" Layla asked.

I had always been of the opinion that if you paid enough attention at a Springsteen show he'd speak directly to you in one song or another. Therefore I had an answer at the ready.

"Definitely *Janey Don't You Lose Heart*," I said. "Not only was it a brilliant acoustic display it made me feel like a moron for almost giving up before I met you."

Adam broke up our moment by announcing that he was ready to get on the road.

"Saddle up, losers we're rolling to the Marriot thanks to the good people at the Seneca-Niagara Casino."

Adam winked at me, and in that wink I knew a secret. He hadn't really won the money; he'd withdrawn it from his bank account. I turned to Mary. She was caught up in a conversation with Rolando. Adam put his finger to his lips to silence me. Ah, what the hell did

I care? We were going to the Marriot.

The room was spectacular, but in the early morning, as I kissed Layla's neck in the darkness of that wonderful room I realized that if I let it happen my life could eventually measure up with my dreams.

"What're you thinking about?" Layla whispered.

"How this is too good to be true," I whispered back. "Last night was monumental."

I returned my attention to her soft, sweet neck, but I stopped all at once because Layla suddenly seemed a million miles away.

"We need to talk about something," she said.

All at once I felt as if I were standing on a chair with a rope around my neck. I quickly considered that the next sentence out of Layla's pretty mouth would displace the chair.

"I sort of get the feeling that you're more afraid than you are in love," she said.

"What're you talking about?" I asked even though I knew exactly what she was saying.

"You say it's too good to be true," she said. "You say that every time I tell you or show you how much I love you."

I propped myself up on my elbow as Layla sat straight up in bed, turning her back to me.

"And I'm afraid too," she said. "But I'm all in. I've hedged my bets. My money is on the table. I've never been more certain about anything, but before we get home, we need to figure this out. Life isn't about chasing Bruce around. Are you scared or do you love me?"

I honestly hadn't seen any of this coming. Therefore I was left without a single word.

"You're forty-four years old. I'm half your age. I get that," Layla said.

Her back remained to me. She reached across and plucked a glass of water from the dresser. She arched her back as she drank. I still couldn't find a word. I knew plenty of words of course. I just had no way of knowing if I'd choose even one right one.

"Because I've been through enough," Layla said. "And I need to know if you have the guts for this. I'm not looking for a father figure. I'm not looking for drama, or trouble, or a man who can't stand up to the challenges. I want your heart and your soul."

Layla laughed nervously.

She turned to face me. In the darkness her beautiful features were masked. I couldn't see the blue of her eyes, or her angelic young face. She was simply a voice in the black. She was asking me for it all, and in the darkness, I was still way too scared to form a sentence.

"I want your love, your children, and your full attention."

I just couldn't answer her.

"Joseph," she whispered. "I sort of need a response here."

I fell back onto the bed. My entire life raced back at me. I had dared to try and love before. Rachael had never truly accepted me. We had played house, and that had crushed me. I thought of the pain of losing Anna and how I'd spent more time in the last year imagining my death instead of my life. How could I explain that I didn't really know what it felt like to actually be loved? The love was extinguished by the fear, and it was so dark.

It was way too dark.

"I think of us in twenty years," I finally whispered back. "And it really does scare me. This doesn't seem real."

Layla didn't answer. Instead, she bent down and picked her newest Bruce shirt and her jeans from the floor.

"Where are you going?" I asked.

"For a walk," she said. "But you better figure it out because I love you, but I'm not strong enough for the both of us. Love is a leap of faith. It's time for you to jump. Ask yourself if you have the fucking stomach to lay your cards on the table, Joseph."

By the time the door swung shut I was up and out of bed, but Layla was moving fast, and it was still way too dark for me to figure out anything quickly.

"Layla!" I called out, but she was out the door and down the hallway. I sank to a sitting position on the inside of the door, naked, alone and scared. I was way too frightened to chase her.

I spent the next twenty minutes of my life collapsed on the floor of the most beautiful hotel room I'd ever been in. It was a room that was paid for by another man. I rolled on the plush carpet, crying for what I'd lost and fearful of the mess I'd make of the love that was right before me. Layla would eventually crush me, of that I was sure. I cried into that carpet, thinking of Bruce singing directly to me the night before, telling me not to lose heart, but what could Bruce do for me now? Layla hadn't come right out and said it, but she left me in the darkness, groping for things I just couldn't grasp.

I finally pulled myself up into a sitting position. From there I was able to find the strength to stand. I'd felt as if I'd reached the valley floor once more. I coaxed myself into standing and found the light switch. I was still standing naked, scared and more than a little alone when I heard the key in the door. Layla came crashing through.

"I met him!" she screamed. "I met Bruce in the lobby!"

She was jumping up and down and her high-pitched screaming actually hurt my ears. The door to the hall was wide open and I was standing there for the world to see, naked as a jaybird. Layla shook her phone and finally held it out to me.

"They stayed here last night! They had the entire eleventh floor. Bruce and Patty were waiting at the elevator and when the door opened they stepped inside. It was just the three of us riding down to the lobby. He was carrying his own bag."

The words were coming fast and furious and they were made more difficult to understand because of the jumping and crying.

The photo on her phone showed Bruce with a sheepish grin, his arms at his side. Layla's eyes were wide and her right hand rested on his shoulder.

"Patty took the picture. My God, they are so perfect. Patty is so nice and so pretty."

Suddenly it occurred to me that I was still naked and still standing in the hall. That realization hit me when an elderly woman shrieked as she saw me. I pulled Layla by the hand and back into room 1206.

"Are you kidding me?" I screamed when we were behind the door. The room was suddenly way too bright. I studied the photo. Bruce was dressed in a black button down shirt and a pair of black jeans. He had a leather bracelet on his right arm. His face held an expression of having been caught.

"We talked!" Layla said. "I told him all about our trip and our quest to meet him. I begged him to wait until I could come and get you, but he said that he had to get back to New Jersey because it'd been a long time since he saw his kids. He said he'd make sure that we got back stage after the last Jersey show!"

The words continued to come fast and furious and tears were streaming down Layla's face.

"I told him how much I loved him and how he changed my life. I told him that I love you so much but that you were being a pussy. I said that! I told Bruce that you were being a pussy! Patty laughed! He finally looked at me, looked up at the elevator lights and said, 'Calm down, Sweetie.' It was so fucking great! Bruce called me Sweetie!"

All at once I fell to the floor again, just inside the door. The only difference being that this time there were arms around me to guide me and the overhead light illuminated everything. Layla ripped her clothes off. The cell phone with Bruce's image blinking back was all but forgotten as we made love just inside the door on that perfectly soft carpet.

"Do you believe it?" she asked afterwards.

"It certainly seems real enough," I answered.

Afterwards Layla offered one simple confession.

"I promise to love you forever, for sure," she said. "But for a minute there, with my eyes closed, you *were* Bruce," she said.

We laughed for a full minute.

And during those precious sixty seconds all of the fear melted away. Layla would be my life. She'd be my companion for this part of the ride. It only took a brief meeting with Bruce to etch it in stone.

CHAPTER 18 – THE SWAMPS OF JERSEY

The restaurant at the Marriot was alive with chatter about the E Street Band spending the night. Our waitress, a pretty girl named Maria, actually whispered that she had served breakfast to Little Steve and his wife, Maureen.

"He left a hundred dollar tip for a twenty-three dollar tab," Maria whispered.

Yet Layla was the star of the show. She showed total strangers the photo of her with Bruce. Mary studied the image for nearly twenty minutes, tears forming in the corner of her eyes.

"It shows me that the trip is blessed from above," she said. "We are a group of malcontents, for sure, but God's light is upon us."

I wasn't sure about all of that, but as I sopped up the remnants of the over-easy eggs with a piece of rye toast I couldn't help but smile. We were on a mission. No matter what happened on the rest of the trip we had been wildly successful.

During the breakfast something suddenly occurred to me. It seemed as if there was a certain sudden twist of life captured in Adam's and Mary's eyes. They glanced knowingly, smiling nearly non-stop even when there didn't seem to be a good reason for their glee.

"Are you two doing it?" Rolando asked.

Apparently he had also noticed the synergy.

"No! Dear God!" Mary called out. "But we have a couple of announcements, for sure. We'll talk about it on our way to the New Jersey."

"I have an announcement too," Rolando said. He leaned back in his chair and used a parry knife to pick the bacon out of his teeth. He didn't seem to be in the least bit interested in Mary's announcement.

"I know it doesn't mean anything in the grand scheme of things," Rolando said. "But I'm going to make some big changes. I'm going to drop seventy-five pounds. When the trip is over I'm going to quit drinking. I'm going back to school, and I'm going to shower every fucking day."

We all laughed, but the fact that Mary and Adam were nodding at the exact same speed told me that something was brewing in their collective minds. They had a plan for Rolando. They were acting like the proud parents of all of us.

Inside the truck we broke down the rest of the trip. Door-to-door we were looking at our longest stretch of highway. It would take us a little over eight hours to go from the Marriot in Toronto to the Newark Hilton at Penn Station in Newark, New Jersey where we'd be a mere two blocks from the Prudential Center Arena where Bruce would perform for three straight nights.

"We're all going to meet him there," Mary said confidently. Then she glanced at Adam once more. "Our lives will be changed forever with this trip."

Rolando was in the driver's seat for the trip out of Canada. He also chose the tunes for the trip, settling on a Bruce bootleg tape from *The Ghost of Tom Joad* tour. Rolando was at full voice, belting out the racy lyrics to *Red-Headed Woman*.

The line of cars at the border station at the Peace Bridge allowed us plenty of time to get our paperwork together. We weren't carrying anything back from Canada to the States even leaving behind the last of the Triple X beer, much to Rolando's dismay.

"Fucking Bin Laden ruined it for all of us," Rolando yelled out as we settled into the line three cars from the interview station. "I used to run into Canada on a weekly basis to see the girls at the ballet."

"Ballet?" Layla asked me.

"Strip joints," I said.

"And now we have to line up like criminals and be searched everywhere we go. Fucking Bin Laden."

Rolando lit a cigarette. He gathered up all the copies of identification that Mary arranged for him. When we got to the window Rolando snuffed out his cigarette and extended the documentation to a man dressed in a uniform. The man looked exactly like Jeff Daniels from the *Dumb and Dumber* movies.

"Where are you coming from?" the guard asked Rolando.

"Toronto," Rolando answered.

"What was your business in Toronto?"

"We went to the concert," Rolando said.

"What concert?" the guard asked.

"Bruce," Rolando said.

The guard was definitely messing with us. All at once I got the feeling that we were going to be exiting the vehicle. We had gained entrance into Canada without a problem, but something was amiss in this guy's eyes as he attempted to stall us in returning to our own country. He appeared to be one of those gentlemen who enjoyed handling a badge, and he was speaking directly to a man who had little patience for men of authority. I was hoping that Rolando's personality change was already in full gear. Why had we allowed Rolando to drive first?

"Who's Bruce?" the guard asked.

"Bruce Springsteen," Rolando said. "Have you been living under a rock since 1975?"

Mary groaned and leaned across the seat in an effort to diffuse the situation, but it was too late.

"All right, smart guy. Pull it over there."

We were ushered out of the truck and into a room that resembled the control room at NASA. Every person was in full uniform, complete with a nasty facial expression that told us that they were in charge. We were told to wait in a bank of chairs that looked out to the bridge.

"We'll call your name in a few minutes. Our guards are working through a shift change."

"This is bullshit," Rolando muttered. "Bruce who?"

I knew, deep in my heart that the best course of action was to just sit quietly and wait for the officers to do their job. I flashed a warning to Mary and she immediately went to work on calming Rolando down a bit. Adam, in the meantime, headed off to a quiet corner to make a couple of telephone calls. He always seemed to be on the phone.

As it turned out, our wait wasn't a very long one at all.

"Come with us," a tall, black man said as he pointed to the center of Rolando's chest. Adam closed his phone and made an effort to intercede.

"What's going on?" Adam asked flashing his big boy grin.

"There's a warrant for your friend's arrest," the black man said. "He's charged with assault in Buffalo."

"Oh no, Ralph!" Mary called out.

"The complaint was filed by John Littlefield," the officer said as he glanced at his clipboard.

"My fucking stepfather," Layla whispered.

Rolando stood before the officer. He held his hands out in front of him as if he were waiting to be cuffed, and to our surprise, the officer willingly obliged. Right there, in the center of the huge room with a whole lot of people looking on, Rolando was read his rights.

"Where are you taking him?" Mary asked through tears.

"The holding station in Erie County," the officer said. "Buffalo."

Rolando was led away. Just before he disappeared from view he turned back and looked at us.

"You see what the fuck happens when I decide to live life the right way?" he asked.

Back in the truck Layla was nearly inconsolable. She screamed out, calling her stepfather every name in the book.

"He attacked me!" she cried. "He treated me like a fucking two-dollar whore, and he has the gall to have Rolando arrested? Why do we do things like this to each other? Why is the world so screwed up? Why? Joseph, why?"

I certainly couldn't answer that question, but it felt natural to slip my arms around Layla to just hold her until the crying stopped.

We made our way back into the country and instead of following the route to New Jersey we headed off to Buffalo again. There wasn't any way that we'd leave Rolando behind.

"Give me your phone, please," Layla said. "I'm calling my mother."

I wasn't sure it was the best idea in the world, but I handed over the phone, and with trembling hands Layla punched in the numbers. She took a deep breath and wiped a tear clear of her left eye.

"You knew he was raping me," Layla said very calmly into the phone. "You let it happen. You know he deserved to get the shit kicked out of him, and now you're letting them arrest Rolando."

Layla seemed suddenly calm and controlled. I couldn't imagine the hate in her heart, but she was hiding it from her mother.

"Seriously?" she asked. "That's your final answer, mother?"

Layla closed the phone without another word. She handed it back to me. All at once Layla broke into a belly laugh that shocked me.

"You know what she said?" Layla asked.

I shrugged.

"She said, *life's not fair, kiddo.*"

The words stuck in my head for the entire rest of the trip. *Life's not fair, kiddo,* Indeed.

***

As we waited in the lobby of the Erie County Holding Center I worked on a note to Anna. The word of the day was *liege* which meant loyal and faithful, and with Adam gazing over my shoulder as I typed I wrote a quote from Lao Tzu: *If you do not change direction you may end up where you're heading.*

"Where do you come up with this shit?" Adam asked.

"I read a lot," I said.

"Evidently," Adam said. "For me it's sort of becoming real clear. You want to hear the gospel according to Adam?"

"This oughta' be good," I laughed.

"Three things," Adam said. "*Life is love, time is short, and money doesn't mean shit.*"

"It means shit if you don't have any," I said.

Adam shook me off.

"Not one great thing we got on this trip was the result of having money," he said. "It made a couple of things a little easier, but it's not what made us smile."

"I like the *life is love,*" Layla said. "It's better than *life isn't fair, kiddo.*"

We sat in silence for a little more than a half an hour. I was holding Layla, Mary had her hand coupled with Adam's. All around us there was absolute chaos as police officers hustled new prisoners in to be printed and processed. The soda machine was making sounds, the place smelled of sweat, and failure. I took in every sound. I listened to the feet hitting the tile floor, and the conversations between the officers and they people they had captured. The four of us simply sat in silence. We were calm and centered. We had found out what it took to live our lives.

"*Life is love; time is short; and money isn't shit,*" I said.

Adam nodded.

Moments later, Rolando was ushered through the door. We had posted his bail. He was a free man.

"The dogs on Main Street howl!" He called out.

"Because they understand," the rest of us answered.

"We're heading for the swamps of Jersey!" Rolando cried out.

Chapter 19 – The Door that Holds the Throne

The fatigue of the trip took hold. Mary was in the driver's seat and the rest of us settled in, mostly sleeping for the next couple of hours. Layla was tight to my left shoulder, and the feel of her skin on my skin was comforting and exciting at the same time. I considered life before her and the despair of living alone just missing Rachael and Anna. It dawned on me that I'd found a great deal of what I'd been searching for. I kissed Layla on her forehead, and she purred like a kitten and smiled without opening her eyes.

Rolando was also fast asleep. We'd all gotten used to his incessant snoring and the other noises that he was all too willing to share. He'd taken the arrest and his time in the holding center in stride. I was pretty sure that he felt a lot better about things as well.

It was Adam who had me worried. It seemed as though he'd been on the cell phone for the better part of three days, and he had not shared a single thing with me. Mary was most likely his confidant, but neither of them appeared to be overly enthusiastic in talking about what was going on.

After my nap, I carefully shifted Layla to the side, putting a small pillow behind her pretty head, and I made my way two seats back towards Rolando. My big friend had also finished his rest, and he pulled back the tab on an ice cold beer. I sat in the seat directly in front of him.

"One of the lyrics that always made my skin jump is from *Born in the U.S.A.*," I said. "Bruce sings about being ten years down the road with nowhere to go."

Rolando considered the words for a moment.

"I always a wanted a plan," I said. "When Bruce sang those words back in the '80's, I considered him to be speaking directly to me. I always say it over and over," I said. "Nowhere to go."

"It looks like you've got a plan now," Rolando said as he motioned to Layla.

"That's always been the plan," I said. "I've always been looking for someone to love my stupid ass."

"I always figured I was better off alone," Rolando said.

"Which calls to mind another Bruce lyric," I said. "In *Two Hearts* he sings about two being better than one when it comes to hearts."

Rolando looked a bit confused. He wasn't sure if he'd ever heard that song. I would make sure he did the next time I switched the CD.

"Do you believe in God?" Rolando asked.

The question wasn't exactly out of left field as I'd figured that sooner or later Rolando would arrive at such a place. He'd been doing a lot of heavy thinking, maybe for the first time in his life, and it was *the* natural question.

"Of course I do," I said, "but it isn't an easy question, is it?"

"Bruce opened the concert with that question the other night. He said something about knocking on the door that holds the throne. Is that what he's talking about? Is he trying to get answers from above?"

I laughed.

"Like the rest of us, Bruce spends a lot of time thinking about it," I said. "The thing about it is that you have to answer it for yourself."

Rolando held the beer to his lips until he drained it. He crumpled the can and nodded in the direction of the cooler. I grabbed him a new one.

"It's certainly been sort of fucked up trying to wedge God in," Rolando said. "I was sort of up against it from day one, but after seeing everyone else on this trip it occurs to me that I've always been looking for an excuse to behave like an asshole."

"That's the way it goes," I said. "Some people don't catch themselves until it's too late."

Rolando took another healthy drink of the cold beer. He burped loudly.

"Do you think I can be saved?" he asked.

"It's about faith," I said. "You need faith in something, but you gotta' find it in yourself."

Rolando laughed.

"A bunch of fucking fortune cookies," he said. "Between your words, Bruce's words and Mary's words I'm one confused motherfucker. Sometimes I'm right there with you, and then I feel it slipping back into my old excuses."

"*Faith is the art of holding onto things your reason has accepted, in spite of your changing moods.* That's from C.S. Lewis."

"Whoever the fuck he is," Rolando said.

Our conversation was interrupted by Mary's right hand turn into the parking lot of a Wal-Mart parking lot. Surprisingly it was Adam who made his way to the microphone. He turned down the volume on *Incident on 57th Street* and cleared his voice to get all of our attention.

"Testing one, two," he said.

Layla stirred awake and it was a little comical as she panicked when she didn't find me right next to her. She hopped up quickly and headed for the seat beside me.

"My job is to set up the next leg of our little tour," Adam said. "If I don't do this right Mary will skin me alive, so hang with me."

Adam glanced down at the note in his hand. The fact that he was working with Mary to organize our efforts was surprising enough, but they were being way too secretive.

"Our hotel is less than a mile from the arena," Adam said. "We'll arrive in New Jersey six hours before the first of three nights of shows so we aren't going to have a lot of time, but there's one thing we must do."

Adam's voice rose and he glanced in Mary's direction. She offered a confirming nod.

"As Joseph knows Bruce spent a lot of time, in his younger days, playing at the Stone Pony in Asbury Park. We need to get there to pay homage. One of the things we have all come to realize on this trip is that we can't just arrive at where we want to be without acknowledging our past."

"Fuck the past," Rolando called out.

"And that would be a mistake," Mary said as she grabbed the microphone from an obviously relieved Adam. "If we condemn our past as garbage without addressing our pain we are doomed to repeat it."

There wasn't a sound on that truck in that moment following our comprehension of Mary's words.

"So the Stone Horse it is," Layla said.

"Stone Pony!" Mary, Adam and I all answered at once.

Wonderful Mary took over the next ten minutes with a history of the Stone Pony telling us all about the original owners Jack Roig and Butch Pielka. She told us that the name of the club came to Pielka in a dream, and that one of the first house bands was The Blackberry Booze Band that featured Steven Van Zandt and Southside Johnny.

"The show that put the Stone Pony on the national map was the 1976 Memorial Day show that featured the Asbury Jukes, Bruce, and Ronnie Spector. But the great times didn't last, and as the city crumbled so did the finances of the club. Jack and Butch don't own the place anymore but it is alive and well as a museum to the music."

Rolando, true to his nature, was a little bored with the history of it all, but he didn't completely miss the message. We were all crowded together in two rows of seats. Mary set the microphone down so that we were all speaking on even ground.

"So the Pony went from glory to shambles and back to glory," Rolando said. "Say, when was the first time Bruce ever played *Thunder Road* in concert?"

"February-fifth in 1975," Mary said. "He sang it at the piano at The Main Point in Bryn Mawr, Pennsylvania."

Rolando laughed at Mary's quick response.

"First song you ever heard Bruce sing live?" Layla said to me.

"September-twenty-fourth, 1984," I said. "He opened with *Born in the USA.* His second song that night was *Out in the Street.* It was at Memorial Auditorium in Buffalo."

The memory of those moments swept across my mind. Layla wasn't even born then. Adam and Mary had been sitting beside me that night. The connection was overpowering given what had happened along the way on this trip.

"You know what it's all about?" Adam asked. He gained his feet and paced in a short space heading towards the back row of seats. He put on his best Bruce-preacher voice.

"It's about love and faith and hope and desperation and rage and forgiveness and loyalty and sadness and despair and spirituality and God. It's all a big-ass circle of life. We can't retreat and there's no surrender."

Adam then went on to recite the lyrics to *No Surrender.* He did it letter perfect. I almost fell to the floor of the truck.

"And God," he whispered.

My phone chimed as a text arrived from Anna.

"Quote of the day," she wrote. "It's from Mother Theresa. *We need to find God and he cannot be found in noise and restlessness.*"

I read the quote for all to hear as a stray tear found its way down my face.

"My biggest problem," Rolando softly said, "Is that I fear that one day I'll meet God and he'll sneeze and I won't know what to say."

We all laughed, but Rolando backed it up with what he remembered from the opening of *We Take Care of Our Own.*

"'I'm gonna' knock at the door that holds the throne.'"

Mary took control of the moment by handing each one of us a beer. We all waited to turn back the tab.

"There's a new day coming," she said. "As Clarence said right after the last show he ever played with the band as they left Buffalo in November of 2009: 'This could be the start of something big.'"

Chapter 20 – Never Looking Back

The inside of the Stone Pony was indeed a museum to rock and roll. We were searching for photos of Bruce, of course, but the walls of the club were filled with so much more. Mary was the curator of our little walk around, showing us old photos of Little Steven, Nils, John Cafferty and Southside Johnny.

"Can you imagine how alive this scene must have been?" she asked excitedly.

Yet we were a group that didn't seem to be in too much of a hurry to visit the past. Layla was squeezing my hand tightly; her eyes were focused on the here and now as she watched a group of new wave performers belting out a loud song that didn't really fit in with the rock and roll image of the place. All at once she shrieked, pointing to a large black and white photo of Springsteen.

"He was so hot."

In the photo Bruce was holding his guitar by the neck. His dark, piercing eyes reflected a deep pain that seemed to need release. Layla had shrieked because Bruce's face was a young face, surely no older than twenty-five or six.

"I wish I knew him then," Layla said. "My God what I would have done to him."

"Tell me all about it," Rolando said from over Layla's shoulder. "Don't leave out a single detail."

Mary joined Layla to pay homage to the youth and beauty of the photograph.

"I knew him intimately then through his music," Mary said. "It seems like yesterday. I think of all we shared since then."

We might have gone on reminiscing for an hour had we not been interrupted by Adam who was holding a poster board size flyer.

"Check this out!" he yelled.

I read the headline.

MEET BRUCE & THE E-STREET BAND!!!

"It's a raffle," Adam shouted as the band kicked in to a new song behind us. He grabbed Mary's hand and like a flock of sheep we followed both of them out into the parking lot.

"The tickets are ten bucks apiece," Adam said as we stood under the sign to the Stone Pony. "In the middle of the final New Jersey concert a drawing will be held and the winning ticket will be a VIP pass to enter the backstage area for a meet and greet with Bruce and the other members of the E Street Band. All proceeds from the raffle will benefit the food bank of Northern New Jersey."

By the time Adam had finished reading the flyer we were all jumping up and down.

"It's fate," Mary said. "The prize is for five people. We are destined to win."

Rolando, of course, was skeptical.

"You know how many fucking tickets they're gonna' sell for that raffle?" he asked. "We have a grand left. Are we gonna' spend every nickel to win a stupid raffle? And what will it get us anyway? Do we really need to meet Bruce? Do we?"

The question sat right there in front of all of us.

"Haven't we already found what we needed to find?" Rolando asked. "Didn't we? I'd like to shake marble mouth's hand too, but I'm just saying, we already do understand."

It was an amazing speech coming from a man who started the trip as a foul-mouthed farting machine. We all grew silent as we contemplated what had been said. Right on cue Rolando let go a loud blast of beer-filled air.

"I'm just saying," he said. "I'm already a changed man."

Mary made her way to Rolando. She stood mere inches from his face, and all at once she raised her right hand, gently touching the razor stubble on Rolando's left cheek.

"I hear what you're saying," she whispered. "But I really need to kiss Bruce. I really do. Adam, go pull fifty grand out of the bank. We're winning this raffle!"

***

That night Bruce ended the New Jersey show with a rousing, ten-minute rendition of *American Land*. The song exhausted the sold-out crowd, and as the band took a number of bows before the adoring gathering I kept looking at Bruce as if he were still that young man captured in that nearly forty-year-old photograph. He was just a man. His past defined the man who now stood before us on that stage. He'd survived doubt, fear, loss and gain. He had stood tall and spit in the face of the badlands.

"Thank you," I mouthed to him on that stage. "We'll see you tomorrow."

But Bruce wasn't done.

"I live five minutes away!" he called out. "You want one more song?"

The place went crazy.

"You're the ones who have to get up for work!" Bruce said. "I get to sleep in."

The crowd answered again with a louder cheer.

Bruce sang out the opening line welcoming Rosie into our world for a few moments.

Twenty minutes later we were filing out of the arena, our ears still ringing with the celebration that was *Rosalita*, and our pockets filled with five thousand raffle tickets.

***

I woke early the next morning. My head was pounding as there was residual ringing in my ears from yet another flawless performance. Layla was fast asleep beside me, her naked body pressed close to me. Her pretty face quieted by her slumber. I couldn't take my eyes off of her. Would our love survive the test of time? Could I be the man she needed me to be? I had failed every single test up to now. Was Rolando right? Had we found what we needed to move forward? Could we survive the pain of the past? I thought of Anna, and how much I missed seeing her smile. I was happy. I was sad. I was lost and I was found. Everything I would need to make my life sing was lying in the bed beside me. Was I smart enough not to mess it up? I thought of the raffle ticket, of God, of love and of fear. The love overwhelmed me, but the fear was just as paralyzing.

"Good morning, handsome," Layla said, slowly opening up her eyes and smiling at me. "Are you thinking about how much you love me?"

"As a matter of fact," I whispered.

The ringing in my ears stopped almost instantly. The fear wasn't quite as paralyzing as I thought.

"Wow, you're really limber this morning," she said.

"Yeah, not so bad for an old man," I said.

***

We spent the afternoon in the parking lot of the Brendan Byrne Arena. Rolando had set up our little campsite, placing the lawn chairs in a circle behind the truck. The back gate was open and *Darkness on the Edge of Town* was providing the background music for one more conversation about what we would be doing when we returned to our lives.

"You must really be looking forward to going back to work with your old man," Rolando said to Adam.

"You must be looking forward to your time in jail," Adam responded.

Yet Adam had fielded the question with one eye on Mary. She smiled.

"What the hell is going on?" I asked.

Mary was dressed in full gypsy garb. Little Steven had worn a black bandana last night and Mary had copied the look perfectly. She shrugged as if my question was absolutely without merit.

"Yeah," Rolando said. "There definitely is something going on with you two losers. Mary you let him take fifty grand out for those raffle tickets. You have plans for us, don't you?"

"You're out of your fucking mind," Adam said.

Once more Adam was bailed out of answering the tough questions. About a hundred feet away in the parking lot area, a screaming match broke out. A man, staggering around the back end of an old model Blue Ford Pinto chased after a middle-aged woman who appeared to be dressed in just an over-sized, red tee-shirt.

"I'll fucking kill you, you fucking bitch!" the man shouted.

The woman was in tears yet she made no effort to really get away. We watched as the man grabbed her by her golden hair and swung her back to the car.

"Oh Jesus," Rolando yelled getting up and knocking his chair over in the process. "Get your hands off of her!"

Despite his size Rolando covered the ground quickly. The man sensing that he was about to get what he wanted - a fight - turned to brace himself for Rolando's approach. He wasn't braced quite well enough.

Rolando hit the man in the mid-section, driving him, the beer and the woman straight to the ground.

"Are you a big man?" Rolando screamed. "Does it make you feel better to beat up a woman?"

Rolando sat dead center on the man's chest. The woman scrambled to her feet. To the utter disbelief of all of us she slapped at the back of Rolando's head.

"Leave him alone," the woman cried. "Just leave him alone."

But Rolando would have none of it. He brushed the woman aside with a wave of his hand. The man struggled below him, screaming out drunken words filled with hatred.

"I'm gonna' tell you something," Rolando said. The big man's breathing was uncontrollable. "When you live for yourself, it's hard on everyone else around you."

"Get off me!" The man screamed.

"What are you afraid of?" Rolando screamed at the man. "Tell me that and I'll leave you alone."

"What?" the guy shrieked.

"What are you afraid of?" Rolando screamed again. "Because it's your fear of being a failure that is making you beat this lady."

"You don't know shit!" the guy moaned.

"I know that you're garbage," Rolando said. "I know that you're life is a fucking mess. I know that I should just crush your head because you don't deserve the things you have."

Adam pointed in the direction of a group of men in yellow security jackets who were about a hundred yards away but heading for the scene.

"You better figure it out," Rolando whispered to the guy. "I'm telling you, buddy, one former loser to one present one, you better figure it the fuck out."

Rolando reached his hand out to me and I helped him up and off the man. The woman was on the ground wailing loudly. The men were racing towards us. Mary and Layla had packed up the car and it was running. We jumped in and Mary gunned it just before the men in the bright yellow jackets arrived.

"We're going racing in the streets," Adam called out.

"It's a town full of losers," Rolando cried to the gathering guards. "We're pulling out of here to win."

CHAPTER 21 – THERE'S MAGIC IN THE NIGHT

"Thund*er Road*," Rolando said. "Tell me more about that one."

I settled in a bit, and before beginning the story I reached for a beer and tapped cans with Rolando. We had pulled into another parking lot about a half-a-mile away from the fight scene. Rolando, Layla and I were seated in a semi-circle, sharing a beer.

"Rumor has it that Bruce got the title from an old Robert Mitchum film. He wanted to sing it perfectly like Roy Orbison, but he wasn't thrilled when he heard how his voice sounded on the record."

"It's fucking perfect," Rolando said. "He's a lonely guy looking for comfort, but he's not sure it's there for him. If you didn't know it you'd think he was just about to kill himself before he saw her dress wave on the porch."

"Actually, it's more optimistic than that," I said. "He sings about faith and the fact that there's magic in the night."

Mary opened a lawn chair and pulled it into the circle beside Rolando. She reached for his hand. Rolando allowed Mary to take hold of his hand and glanced down as she traced small fingers around the palm.

"A lot of pain," she whispered.

Obviously Mary's entrance to the circle had been orchestrated because a moment later Adam joined us. The circle was now complete.

"Back before the *Tunnel of Love* Tour a friend of mine from college, Rosie, made her pilgrimage to the Stone Pony in Asbury Park, New Jersey," Mary said. "Rosie's goal was simply to sit at the bar and look at the stage where Bruce played so many nights as he started out. Rosie was lost in the nostalgia and she never noticed the man who sat down on her right and in a gruff voice ordered a bottle of beer. It was a few minutes before Rosie glanced over, but when she did, it struck her that it was Bruce sitting there, also staring forlornly at the stage."

"Get the fuck out of here," Rolando said. "Did she hug him?"

"Nope," Mary said. "She nodded a hello, Bruce nodded back, and then they drank their beer. Rosie never told Bruce how much his music meant to her. Rosie didn't gush over Bruce. She actually didn't do anything more than nod. They just shared a quick moment in a perfect setting."

Mary let the words sink in.

"They just shared a moment that meant a lifetime to Rosie. At the end of this trip that might be all that we have done. We shared some moments."

Mary turned to Adam. He had tears in his eyes.

"All right, what the fuck is going on?" Rolando whispered. "Is Adam dying?"

The long pause before Adam spoke was uncomfortable for all of us. He paused for so long that Layla gasped beside me.

"Life is a series of moments," Adam said. "We don't all get to sit shoulder-to-shoulder with Bruce."

Adam's voice broke, and he bowed his head.

"I thank God for the moments that I've been able to share with the people I love," he said.

At that precise moment it *did* seem to me that Adam was about to tell us that he had some sort of debilitating disease.

"And no matter how hard we try to keep life the same; no matter how hard we try and hold onto the things that matter; they seem to slip away. We forget to keep on loving the things we love. We get wrapped up in a lot of bullshit."

The second long pause sent Rolando into a rage of impatience.

"What the fuck is it?" He asked as he got to his feet. There were strains of tears in Rolando's booming voice.

Mary whispered the words that Adam was searching for.

"Adam wants to take care of his own," she said.

Adam nodded and smiled. There was no mistaking the emotion burning through him as he spoke.

"I'm not going back to work for my father," he said. "When we saw Bruce in Pittsburgh I made up my mind to make some major changes. When Bruce sang *Land of Hopes and Dreams* and the line about needing a good companion, I made a series of real decisions, and it involves all of you. I'm hoping that you'll accompany me on the next little while during our journey."

Rolando tipped back in his chair and I considered that if he went over backwards it would ruin the moment. He swung his beer can back and forth in front of him as he called out.

"If you don't tell us what the fuck you're talking about, I swear to

God I'm gonna' pummel the both of you."

Adam gave Mary a thumbs-up sign.

"Adam wants to know if you'll spit in the face of the badlands with him."

"I'm warning you," Rolando said. He stood up.

Mary stood and her dressed waved as she motioned Rolando back to his seat.

"Adam worked out a deal with his father. Over the course of the last few days Adam's father bought his son out of the company."

I couldn't help it; I stood and clapped and moments later Rolando and Layla joined me.

"A major part of the deal was a 30-acre piece of property in the Town of East Aurora," Mary said. "It's a parcel of land that has five homes on it. The houses were built less than ten years ago, and they are each a little less than 3,000 square feet."

"That's where I went when you were at the Anchor Bar," Adam said. "They're beautiful homes," Adam said. "They're all walking distance from one another."

"Adam put the money down to buy the land. There's a home for Joseph and Layla. There's a home for Rolando. There's one for me and one for Adam."

"I ain't real bright," Rolando called out. "That's only four."

"And there's a home for Rachael and Anna."

The wave of emotion that was bubbling beneath the surface came rushing forward. I made a motion to stand, but feeling as if I were going to faint again, I stumbled back to the seat.

"Rachael and Anna have already accepted the offer," Mary called out. "Are the rest of you in? Is there anyone alive out there?"

Rolando was the first to reach Adam. He grabbed his friend in a huge bear hug that looked like it was crushing ribs.

"I hate to give up my rat's nest apartment," Rolando said, "but I'll join you."

Rolando kissed Adam on both cheeks.

"There's more," Mary whispered. It was a loud, teasing whisper that made us all laugh. "There were three additional purchases worked out. Rolando Arroyo is now the proud owner of a Mobil gas station and repair shop. Joseph and Layla are the proud owners of a combination convenience store and breakfast diner. I will be working with Rachael, and Anna, at a health and wellness spa called *Mary's Place*, of course, after the Bruce song."

Adam's face changed from despair to delight as he realized that we were all in. I took a moment to glance at Layla; there were tears streaming down her face. I was searching for the right words to say. What could possibly be said to a man who'd just set all of us up for the rest of our lives? If life were about building upon moments, we were now in one hell of a spot.

"What're you going to be doing?" Rolando asked Adam.

"Not a fucking thing," Adam said. "I'm going golfing for the rest of my days. You didn't think I'd cut a deal where I'd have to ever work again, did you?"

"How much cash did you get out of the old fuck?" Rolando asked.

"Enough," Adam said. "In fact, I got way more than enough. I'd like to make money off the businesses, but whatever. We're gonna' be together."

I headed for the truck and the sound system. I wasn't real sure what to say to Adam so I decided that we needed a sing-a-long. For the next few minutes the speakers cackled and scratched as in the middle of a New Jersey parking lot we sang ourselves silly to the poetry that was *The Promised Land.*

We rose and fell together, crucifying the song, but believing the message. We took each word into our hearts; screaming them loudly, crying out for the world to hear.

"We're gonna' make it, you worthless bastards!" Adam bellowed out. He was laughing and crying all in a single sound. Rolando tackled Adam and sat down hard on his chest as he'd done to the wife-beater just an hour ago.

"Do you feel the love?" Rolando screamed as he buried Adam's body beneath his own.

"Get the fuck off me," Adam laughed. "Or I'm taking your house back."

I kissed Layla hard and wiped a few of the tears from her face. I just know that they were tears that had been building from the very first moment when her disgusting stepfather crawled on top of her.

"Magic in the night," I whispered.

***

As we prepared for the third and final concert in New Jersey Mary recapped the numbers for us. She was on the microphone in the center aisle of the truck. She had turned her hair bright red for the final show. She reasoned that she was going to meet Bruce after the show and that Bruce was partial to red-headed women.

"We saw the band in Cleveland, Buffalo, Pittsburgh, Toronto and the great state of New Jersey. We've watched six wonderful concerts with one more to go. We've heard everything from *Blinded by the Light* to *We are Alive*. In less than an hour, on the classic rock radio station they are going to interrupt the endless playing of Bruce to announce the winning number and we are going to be holding the magic ticket."

Mary glanced down at the dangling gold bracelets on her arm as though she were looking at a watch.

"A few hours from this very moment we will be shaking hands with Bruce Springsteen."

"I've already met him," Layla said and we all laughed.

Yet Mary had more on her mind. We were all anxious for our new lives to begin at the plantation in East Aurora, but Mary wanted us to go in with a clean slate of sorts.

"We have to clean some things up," she said. She bowed her head. "Something that Rolando shouted at the man who was beating his girlfriend or wife has stuck with me."

It struck me that despite our glee with our new living arrangements we certainly needed to listen to Mary at that moment.

"Rolando screamed, 'What are you afraid of?' to that guy. And it occurred to me, last night, after the show, that the true enemy of love is fear."

I was half-expecting Rolando to shout out something, but his head was riveted to the floor of the truck.

"I've spent years in fear," she said. "I feared that the love I felt for Ralph was the only love that was there for me. I was afraid that if I didn't allow him to punch my teeth in that there wouldn't be anyone there to feel anything for me. Being punched was better than being ignored."

"And I feared failure," Rolando said as he took the microphone from Mary. "I sabotaged everything I ever did because I didn't think I was smart enough, or skinny enough, or handsome enough. I never wanted to fail, so I thought up reasons not to try, and then I gathered all the things I had going for me, put them in a huge pile in front of me, and shit and pissed all over them. I ain't fucking doing that anymore."

I wasn't sure what was expected of me, but true to form, I was afraid to take my turn. Did we need to confess before we won the raffle to meet Bruce?

"I loved being a kid," Adam said. He held the microphone low and didn't rise from his seat. "I loved being good at sports and having the girls love me because my old man had money and because I'm built like a Greek god."

I smiled and when I looked around I saw that we were all smiling.

"But I was fearful of being a man and being judged by my old man. Of course I was going to fail. In his eyes, I've been a failure since the day I was born. I ain't apologizing to no one anymore. Because now I'm a man."

We were less than a half an hour away from finding out if we held the ticket that would put us in front of Bruce. The two people left to speak of failure were sitting together in the same seat. I wasn't sure what we would say. I didn't know if I'd be able to speak at all.

"I love love," Layla said. "But I've always been scared of it." Her voice cracked, and a sob escaped as she let go of my hand for the first time all day and found her feet. She paced the center aisle of the truck. "When my vile, disgusting stepfather got off of me he said the same thing every time. He said, 'Remember, little girl, I love you.'"

The tremendous rage building inside me was pushed away by the smile that Layla offered in place of the pain.

"Love confused me. I was afraid of it, but I'm not afraid anymore." She looked directly at me. "I love love again."

And there wasn't any mistaking who was next. All eyes turned to me as Layla handed me the microphone. At that precise moment everything built inside me, and the tidal wave of emotion that was cresting in the spot behind my eyes threatened to blow a hole in the center of my forehead. I actually believed I was about to pass out again, but the words just started to come out.

"I fear pain," I whispered. "I fear loss and grief. I'm so scared of everything that through the years I've wondered if there was anything I could offer to anyone. I couldn't help Rachael. I lost myself in Bruce. I've had lousy jobs, horrible days, restless nights, and haunted dreams. You've all had very specific fears," I said. "I just feared *living*. In fact, if Bruce hadn't toured this year, I might have shot myself. Now I wake up with a smile on my face. Every moment is special, and the love overwhelms me. For years I've searched, and I'll probably never stop looking, but right now I think I can relax a little. Fuck fear."

My words hung in the air. I dropped the microphone at my feet. I thought of Layla as my wife. I considered Rachael and Anna living next door. I could almost picture Rolando running the gas station down the street. We could make it work.

"Can we set our fears aside?" Mary whispered. "Can we live happily ever after?"

Mary went to the grey box and retrieved the raffle tickets. We had five thousand chances.

"What if we don't win?" Layla asked.

Mary handed tickets to each of us. Adam turned up the volume on the rock and roll station. They were teasing the fact that a lucky group of five would have their dreams come true.

"We've already won," Rolando said.

Ten minutes later the winning ticket was pulled.

"The moment that you've been waiting for," the announcer said. "If you have the winning ticket you have ten minutes to call the station. The winning number is 547323."

I spent a moment watching everyone scrambling through the tickets they held in their hands. Rolando was throwing the red tickets to the floor of the truck, growling as he realized that his series of tickets had him nowhere near the winning sequence. Layla was also moving quickly, bursting with excitement as she searched and searched for the right combination.

"What was the number?" Adam asked. "I can't fucking remember anything?"

"547323," I said. "But don't worry about it, you don't have it."

"Why would you say that?" Adam asked.

I held up the very first ticket that I had in my hand.

"Because I do."

Chapter 22 – Moving Thru the Dark

On the way into the arena my cell phone buzzed. I brought it to my ear and shouted hello as I shifted my feet in step with Layla who was holding my left hand. We were in perfect rhythm with the crowd of people who were entering the gates. I glanced up at the marquee that announced that it was Bruce Springsteen and the E Street Band on tap for the evening.

"Hello?"

"Hi Joseph," Anna said. "We're gonna' be living next door to you!"

"I know, baby," I said. "That's awesome."

"It's my turn," Anna said. "I know you're going to see Bruce, but I have a quote and a word."

"I'm ready," I said.

Layla was guiding me through the crowd, angling her body to avoid making contact with any of the Bruce fanatics negotiating for space through the gate.

"This is from Karl Augustus Menninger," Anna said. "*Fears are educated into us and can, if we wish, be educated out.*"

The quote actually left me searching for my next breath of air. Was it possible that Mary was feeding Anna the quotes?

"Our word of the day is *magnificent*," Anna said. "And you know what that means. Have a great time, Joseph. I love you."

"I love you too," I said.

We were on our way to another Bruce concert. We held the winning ticket to meet the man, and I was surrounded by love. Life was perfect.

We found our seats in the lower bowl of the arena. Once again we were less than fifty feet from the stage and as had been our costume we bowed before Adam for scoring the tickets.

"I'm going to find a security guard," Mary said. "I'll show him the winning ticket and find out what we need to do after the show."

I wanted to take in every second of the night. I let my eyes dance across the arena every few minutes and watched the place fill up with people. The crowd was a mix of the old and the new. There were certainly senior citizens in the crowd, but there were also a lot of young people wearing real old concert shirts. A girl of about fourteen was wearing the classic *Born to Run* shirt that pictured Bruce and Clarence leaning on one another. I pointed the girl out to Layla who offered up a terrific smile. "We aren't the only ones obsessed with the Boss," she said.

Rolando and Adam stood off to the side with half-empty beer cups in their hands. They were also scanning the crowd, taking in every moment.

"Okay," Mary called out when she returned. "I talked with security."

Mary was forced to yell out due to the cheering crowd as the lights dimmed, signaling that Bruce would be on stage in a moment.

"When *Tenth-Avenue Freeze-Out* starts the guards are going to come and get us and escort us backstage. The band will meet with us for a few moments and we'll pose for a few photos for the newspaper."

Anna had to shout the last few words because the band was making their way to the stage. I screamed out Steven's name and waved to him as he found his position. It almost looked as if he were staring right back at me.

The first blast of sound was unmistakable to the older Springsteen fans in the crowd. The band was going to start out the night with the lights up. Bruce and Nils were side-by-side as Bruce hammered out the wonderful guitar solo to the 1978 version of *Prove it All Night*. By the time he sang the line about dreams coming true, the five people who were about to meet him were in tears.

Time passed quickly as we rode the wave of emotion and sang the songs right along with Bruce who once more was proving that he was more like a jukebox than a man. The lights flickered and then dimmed and Bruce raised his eyes to the bank of lights directly over the stage.

"We having a problem?" he asked as he shared a laugh with Steven. The moment passed and Bruce sang *Jack of All Trades* from the *Wrecking Ball* record.

The sentiment behind the beautiful words weren't lost on Mary or Adam who were holding tightly to one another. Rolando was swaying in time to the ballad with his right fist raised high above his head.

As the night moved along the crowd grew even more boisterous. Bruce relied heavily on the *Born to Run* record and he even threw in a rousing rendition of *Glory Days* that had the crowd singing along with every howl.

"This might be the best show yet," Rolando cried out.

"You say that every time," I answered.

As usual I kept the song count in my head. It was already past eleven o'clock at night and since the band was on their twenty-seventh song I knew that we were reaching the end of our trip. The very last song would be *Tenth-Avenue Freeze-Out* that included a tribute to Clarence, and acknowledging the past love while searching for the future peace. We wouldn't be seeing the song from our seats. Mary tapped me on the shoulder and pointed to the two men who'd come to get us safely backstage. The men were dressed in yellow security vests and were holding radios speaking to people near the side of the stage.

"This is fucking happening," Rolando shouted. "I'm coming to shake your hand, marble-mouth!"

Bruce and Steven danced side-by-side. Clarence's nephew Jake was blitzing the saxophone solo, and we all knew what was coming next. Bruce would raise his hand to the roof of the arena and pay tribute to his lifelong friend. Together we would all acknowledge the pain in our lives, and at that very moment, working together we would vow to keep trying to live the right way.

"Let's go," the man said to me. The man was obviously annoyed with his place in life and it didn't seem as if he were sharing in the magical moment.

"You wanna' meet the band or not?" he asked impatiently.

We hugged the aisle following the two men down the steps towards the back of the stage. Bruce raised his hand as the crowd roared in appreciation of Clarence. Bruce thrust his hand high in the air and it brought even louder cheers. We walked close to the edge of the stage. Bruce's raised arm went into the air once more. I tripped into the back of Adam and he pushed back at me. The crowd roared again, and then it happened.

The lights went out.

Having seen the band seven times in two weeks we instantly knew that it wasn't part of the show.

"We have power failure!" the man with the security vest screamed into his hand-held radio. The place went completely dark. It was like being trapped in the world's biggest, noisiest cave. The music, of course, had abruptly stopped. Bruce's microphone had gone dead as well but in the dark I could hear him calling out to all of us, trying to keep us calm in the face of utter despair.

"Bomb!" someone screamed from the upper bowl and that was when the absolute tidal wave of bedlam hit.

"What the fuck?" Rolando asked. "Stay close. We have to get out of here together!"

Yet the wave of people was absolutely terrifying. I heard a woman scream, and then I felt myself tumbling forward after taking a straight kidney shot. As I reached for the railing thinking that it was to my right, I lost track of Layla's hand. There were lights from people's cell phones offering a bit of illumination but as I moved forward I was hit again and this time I knew that I was about to hit the ground. I went down three steps, someone stepped firmly into the center of my back and I cried out. It occurred to me that I was going to die on the floor of the arena, one of ten, or twenty, or thirty people who was trampled underfoot of his fellow man.

All at once I was raised by the very center of my shirt and my head came off the concrete floor

"Get the fuck up!" Rolando screamed.

"Where's Layla?" I asked.

"We're all heading towards the exit," Rolando said. He was half-carrying and half-pushing me forward. "Just keep your feet moving!"

"But where is she?" I asked.

"With Adam," Rolando said, but in my heart I knew that he was lying. He had no idea where Layla was or if she was all right.

The wave of panic took control. I felt the urge to just stop moving, or to throw-up, or to pass out, something.

"One step in front of the other," Rolando cried. "I'll carry you, brother, if I have to."

And it turns out he had to. The blood rushed from my head and I fainted straight away into his strong arms.

***

The piercing pain in my back brought me back to life. It was strange enough because even though I'd been out for a few minutes I was right back in the center of the turmoil. We had made it to the sidewalk outside the arena, but there was still panic in the air. My first visual was of a blue and white USA Today newspaper box that was directly above my head, and then I saw Mary's wonderful face and that blazing red hair.

"Are you okay?" she whispered.

I sat up and took stock. From ground level I saw people running clear of the arena.

"Did we all get out?"

Mary nodded but I knew she was lying as well.

"Where's Rolando? He carried me out. Where's Adam? Please God, where's Layla?"

The river of tears flowed down my cheeks and Mary held me as if I were a newborn baby.

"We're all going to be just fine," she said. "You'll see, Joseph. No matter what happened in there, we will all survive. Love will always allow us to survive."

I didn't need Mary's fortune-telling words. I needed to touch Layla. I needed to kiss her pretty face, and to hold her again. I cried out as I struggled to my feet.

The power was still off as the inside of the arena was black. Four policemen were standing at the main door ushering the crowd out as sirens pierced the warm night air.

"Rolando and Adam went back in to find her," Mary said. "I told them we'd wait right here for them."

I was back on my feet. The pain in my back nearly forced me straight down to the sidewalk.

"I need to find her," I said. "She's my life."

Mary was about to fight me on it. I knew every single thing about the woman and how she reacted in every situation. I waited for her hands to reach out to grab me, but for the very first time, in a long time, Mary surprised me. Instead of trying to stop me, Mary stepped aside and allowed me to pass. I ran in as nameless people raced out.

"Back off," one of the cops said as he raised his arm to halt my approach.

"Fuck you. Sir," I said. I ducked under his arm and headed straight back into the darkness.

A man with a bullhorn was yelling for people to remain calm. There were still thousands of people trapped in the hallway leading to the open doors. The anguished screams were deafening. I took stock of what I could smell; sweat, blood, and even piss. I struggled through all of it, wedging myself into tight spaces between the flesh of a man and a heavyset woman. Everywhere I looked there was darkness, but there were also flashes of light, coming from the phones.

"Just keep your feet," I could almost hear Rolando shouting. I thought of fear and what Anna had spoken to me just before we had entered the arena. I could educate the fear out. I started calling Layla's name at the top of my voice. I cried out as if I were extorting an arena-filled with people to remember to stay on the right course and to fight back against adversity, tragedy and pain, as if all of human existence depended upon it.

"Layla! Layla! Layla!" I called out.

***

I found her face-down in a dark, isolated corridor next to a stand where they sell peanuts and beer to the people who just want to spend a few hours figuring out that life can still be lived. I knelt down in front of her motionless body. In the light of my cell phone I saw the cities that Bruce had visited on the tour, printed on the back of the pink shirt. I turned her body in a sweeping motion, and my heart stopped for a moment as I considered the rest of my days without her.

And then she smiled.

"Were you worried about me?" she asked.

I fell on top of her and our tears mixed as our lips met.

Chapter 23 –God Have Mercy on the Man

The diner was completely empty with the exception of the five of us gathered around our table. We spoke of the miracle that no one in the crowd had lost their life in the rampage that had ended the show. A few broken bones and a bunch of scattered bruises, but we were all good to go forward.

"How's the ankle?" Rolando asked Layla. Her casted leg was resting on the chair beside her. We'd spent the entire evening in the emergency room.

"Still broken," she said. "Six weeks from now it's gonna' look like a stick."

"Do you wanna' get on the road today or should we spend another night in Jersey?" Adam asked.

"I want out," Layla said. "We need to start our lives together in our little commune."

I caressed her hand and brought it to my lips. I thought about telling her I loved her for the hundredth time that morning, but I held it in. The waitress was back around with the coffee pot, but I held my hand over the top of my cup.

"No thank-you," I said.

"Adam and I will go check out of the room," Mary said. "The rest of you can relax here. We never met Bruce, but at least we all got out alive."

I stretched my back and felt the pain in the lower region. I grimaced through a smile, and we all glanced to my cell phone as the ringtone blasted *Working on a Dream.* We shared yet another laugh.

"It's Anna," Mary said as she reached for the phone and brought it to her ear.

"Okay! Okay!" Mary said. "We will. I promise. Yes, right now!"

Once more my heart jumped to my throat.

"What is it?"

"Come on," Mary said, "We have to go."

Adam took a hundred dollar bill from his pocket and left it on the table. Mary wasn't talking. She simply ran to the truck in the parking lot and we all followed.

"What the hell is going on?" I screamed at Mary.

"We just have to get there." Mary answered. "Evidently you signed some paperwork with Anna as your emergency contact."

I couldn't think of what might have gone wrong. Was Anna okay? Had something happened to Rachael? Three minutes later we were racing into the front doors of the Marriot.

"Are you Joseph?" the woman behind the desk in the lobby asked. Her nametag said 'Carrie Lynn.' She was a beautiful, vibrant, smiling young woman.

"Yes," I answered. I glanced again at the four trailing behind me. Now Mary was smiling too.

"Follow me," Carrie Lynn said. She led me down the hallway and knocked lightly at Room 100. She stepped out of the way and the door opened slowly. Standing right before the five of us was Bruce Springsteen.

"Are you Joseph?" he asked. "I heard you won the contest last night. Sorry we blew the lights out."

I felt myself going faint again. Bruce extended his hand and I shook it calmly.

"I need you to finish a sentence for me," I said. "The dogs on Main Street howl."

"Because they understand," he said.

Rolando wailed loudly behind me.

And that's when I started to cry, and Bruce just laughed.

www.ingramcontent.com/pod-product-compliance
Lightning Source LLC
Chambersburg PA
CBHW070049260626
47160CB00004B/1147